He stepped in closer and whispered in her ear, "Outside."

For a second, neither of them moved. She could feel the heat of his body and she had an almost overwhelming urge to kiss the finger resting against her lips.

What was it about this man that turned her into a schoolgirl with a crush? She still had no idea what he did in his spare time or whether or not it broke any state or federal laws. And there was the unavoidable fact that acting on any lust would be a conflict of interest.

They were actively on a case, for crying out loud.

So instead of leaning into his touch or wrapping her arms around his waist and pulling him in tight, she nodded and pulled away.

It was harder than she thought it would be.

Dear Reader,

Welcome back to the Great Plains, where dedicated FBI Special Agent Tom Yellow Bird has spent the last ten years of his life rooting out corruption in the judiciary system. After his wife died, Tom put away his dreams of a family and a happily-ever-after and threw himself into his job. He's good at what he does, but fighting crime leaves him with no time for a personal life.

Until the Honorable Caroline Jennings is appointed to a vacant seat in South Dakota and Tom testifies in her courtroom. Suddenly, Tom's dealing with something far outside his job description—attraction. Desire. He wants Caroline with a passion—but how far will he go to keep her?

Caroline has her own secrets. She can't afford to do something foolish like fall for a mysterious, extremely wealthy FBI agent. But when a threat throws her into Tom's arms, she's in no hurry to pull away. What could go wrong? Then she discovers she's pregnant.

Pride and Pregnancy is a sensual story about fighting for your dreams and falling in love. I hope you enjoy reading this book as much as I enjoyed writing it! Be sure to stop by sarahmanderson.com and sign up for my newsletter at eepurl.com/nv39b to join me as I say, Long Live Cowboys!

Sarah

SARAH M. ANDERSON

PRIDE AND PREGNANCY

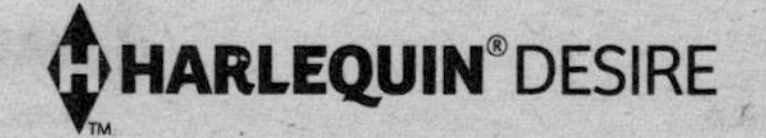

ISBN-13: 978-0-373-83838-7

Pride and Pregnancy

This edition published by arrangement with Harlequin Books S.A.

For questions and comments about the quality of this book, please contact us at CustomerService@Harlequin.com.

Printed in U.S.A.

Sarah M. Anderson may live east of the Mississippi River, but her heart lies out west. *A Man of Privilege* won an *RT Book Reviews* 2012 Reviewers' Choice Best Book Award. *The Nanny Plan* was a 2016 RITA® Award winner for Contemporary Romance: Short.

Sarah spends her days talking with imaginary cowboys and billionaires. Find out more about Sarah's heroes at sarahmanderson.com and sign up for the new-release newsletter at eepurl.com/nv39b.

Books by Sarah M. Anderson

Harlequin Desire

The Nanny Plan
His Forever Family
A Surprise for the Sheikh
Claimed by the Cowboy
Pride and Pregnancy

The Bolton Brothers

Straddling the Line
Bringing Home the Bachelor
Expecting a Bolton Baby

The Beaumont Heirs

Not the Boss's Baby
Tempted by a Cowboy
A Beaumont Christmas
His Son, Her Secret
Falling for Her Fake Fiancé
His Illegitimate Heir
Rich Rancher for Christmas
Billionaire's Baby Promise

Visit her Author Profile page at Harlequin.com, or sarahmanderson.com, for more titles.

To Dorliss Jones and Lynn Orr,
who were wonderful next-door neighbors
to my grandmother and have read every book.
You've been asking for Yellow Bird
for years—so here he is!

One

"Judge Jennings?"

Caroline looked up, but instead of seeing her clerk, Andrea, she saw a huge bouquet of flowers.

"Good Lord," Caroline said, standing to take in the magnitude of the bouquet. Andrea was completely invisible behind the mass of roses and lilies and carnations and Caroline couldn't even tell what else. It was, hands-down, the biggest bunch of flowers she'd ever seen. Andrea needed two hands to carry it. "Where did those come from?"

Because Caroline couldn't imagine anyone sending her flowers. She'd only been at her position as a judge in the Eighth Circuit Court in Pierre, South Dakota, for two months. She had made friends with her staff—Leland, the gruff bailiff; Andrea, her perky clerk; Cheryl, the court reporter who rarely smiled. Caroline had met her neighbors—nice folks who kept to themselves. But at no time had she come into contact with anyone who would send her *this*.

In fact, now that she thought about it, she couldn't imagine anyone sending her flowers, period. She hadn't left behind a boyfriend in Minneapolis who missed her. She hadn't had a serious relationship in… okay, she wasn't going to go into that right now.

For a frivolous moment, she wished the flowers were from a lover. But a lover would be a distraction from the job and she was still establishing herself here.

"It took two men to deliver," Andrea said, her voice muffled by the sheer number of blooms. "Can I set it down?"

"Oh! Of course," Caroline said, clearing off a spot on her desk. The vase was massive—the size of a dinner plate in circumference. Caroline hadn't gotten a lot of flowers over the course of her life. So she could say with reasonable confidence that the arrangement Andrea was carefully lowering onto her desk was more flowers than she had ever seen in one place—excepting her parents' funerals, of course.

She knew her mouth had flopped open, but she seemed powerless to get it closed. "Tell me there was a card."

Andrea disappeared back into the antechamber before returning with a card. "It's addressed to you," the clerk said, clearly not believing Caroline would receive these flowers, either.

Caroline was too stunned to be insulted. "Are you sure? There has to have been a mistake." What other explanation could there be?

She took the card from Andrea and opened the envelope. The flowers had been ordered from an internet company and the message was typed. "Judge Jennings—I look forward to working with you. An admirer," was all it said.

Caroline stared at the message, a sinking feeling of dread creeping over her. An unsolicited gift from a secret admirer was creepy enough. But that's not what this was, and she knew it.

Caroline took her job as a judge seriously. She did not make mistakes. Or, at the very least, she rarely made mistakes. Perfectionism might be a character flaw, but it also had made her a fine lawyer and now made her a good judge.

Once she'd found her footing as a prosecutor, she'd had an impeccable record. When she'd been promoted to judge, she prided herself on being fair in her dealings on the bench, and she was pleased that others seemed to agree with her. The promotion that had brought her to Pierre was a vote of confidence she did not take lightly.

Whoever would spend this much money to send her flowers without even putting his or her name on the card wasn't simply an admirer. Sure, there was always the possibility that someone unhinged had developed an obsession. Every time she read about a judge being stalked back to his or her house—or when a judge and her family in Chicago had been murdered—Caroline resolved to do better with her personal safety. She double-checked the locks on doors and windows, carried pepper spray, and had taken a few self-defense classes. She made smart choices and worked to eliminate stupid mistakes.

But Caroline didn't think this bouquet was from a stalker. When she'd accepted this position, a lawyer from the Justice Department named James Carlson had contacted her. She knew who he was—the special prosecutor who had been chasing down judicial corruption throughout the Great Plains. He'd put three judges in prison and forcibly retired several others from the bench after his investigations.

Carlson hadn't given her all of the details, but he had warned her that she might be approached to take bribes to throw cases—and he'd warned her what would happen if she accepted those bribes.

"I take these matters of judicial corruption seriously," he had told her in an email. "My wife was directly harmed by a corrupt judge when she was younger, and I will not tolerate anyone who shifts the balance on the scales of justice for personal gain."

Those words came back to her now as Caroline continued to stare at the flowers and then at the unsigned note. Those flowers were trying to tip the scale, all right.

Damn it. Of course she knew that people in South Dakota would not be less corrupt than they were in Minnesota. People were people the world over. But despite Carlson's warning, she'd held out hope that he was wrong. He had stressed in his email that he didn't know who was buying off judges. The men he'd prosecuted had refused to turn on their benefactors—which, he had concluded, meant they either didn't know who was paying the bills or they were afraid.

Part of Caroline didn't want to deal with this. Unknown individuals compromising the integrity of the judicial system—that was nothing but a headache at best. She wanted to keep believing in an independent court and the impartiality of the law. Short of that, she didn't want to get involved in a messy, protracted investigation. There was too much room for error, too much of a chance that her mistakes might come back to haunt her.

But another part of her was excited. What this was, she thought as she stepped around her desk to look at the flowers from a different angle, was a case without a resolution. There were perpetrators, there were victims—there was a motive. A crime needed to be solved and justice needed to be served. Wasn't that why she was here?

"How long do we have before the next session starts?" she asked, returning to her chair and calling up her email. She had no proof that this overabundance of flowers had anything to do with Carlson's corruption case—but she had a hunch, and sometimes a hunch was all a woman needed.

"Twenty minutes. Twenty-five before the litigants get restless," Andrea answered. Caroline glanced up at the older woman. Andrea was staring at the bouquet with an intense longing that Caroline understood.

"There's no way I can keep all of these," she said, searching for Carlson's name and pulling up his last email. "Feel free to take some of them home, decorate the office—strew rose petals from here to your car?"

She and Andrea laughed together. "I think I will," the clerk said, marching out of the office in what Caroline could only assume was a quest to find appropriate containers.

Caroline reviewed the emails she and James Carlson had exchanged before she opened a reply and began to type. Because one thing was clear—if this were some nefarious organization reaching out to her, she was going to need backup.

Lots of backup.

Sometimes, Tom Yellow Bird thought, the universe had a sense of humor.

What other explanation could there be when, the very morning he was scheduled to testify in the court of the Honorable Caroline Jennings, he had received an email from his friend James Carlson, informing him that the new judge, one Honorable Caroline Jennings, had received a suspicious bouquet of flowers and was concerned it might be connected to their ongoing investigation into judicial corruption in and around Pierre, South Dakota?

It would be funny if the situation weren't so serious, he thought as he took a seat near the back of the courtroom. This trial was for bank robbery, and Tom, operating in his capacity as an FBI agent, had tracked down the perpetrator and arrested him. The robber had had the bank bags in his trunk and marked bills in his wallet. A cut-and-dried case.

"All rise," the bailiff intoned as the door at the back of the courtroom opened. "The court of the Eighth Judicial Circuit, criminal division, is now in session, the Honorable Caroline Jennings presiding."

Tom had heard it all before, hundreds of times. He rose, keeping his attention focused on the figure clad in black that emerged. Another day, another judge. Hopefully she wasn't easily bought.

"Be seated," Judge Jennings said. The courtroom was full so it wasn't until other people took their seats as she mounted the bench that Tom got his first good look at her.

Whoa.

He blinked and then blinked again. He had expected a woman—the name Caroline was a giveaway—but he hadn't expected *her*. He couldn't stop staring.

She took her seat and made eye contact across the room with him, and time stopped. Everything stopped. His breath, his pulse—everything came to a screeching halt as he stared at the Honorable Caroline Jennings.

He'd never seen her before—he knew that for certain because he'd remember her. He'd remember this *pull*. Even at this distance, he thought he saw her cheeks color, a delicate blush. Did she feel it, too?

Then she arched an eyebrow in what was a clear challenge. Crap. He was still standing, gawking like an idiot, while the rest of the court waited. Leland cracked a huge smile, and the court reporter looked annoyed. The rest of the courtroom was starting to crane their necks so they could see the delay.

So he took his seat and tried to get his brain to work again. Caroline Jennings was the judge on this case and she was his assignment from Carlson—nothing more. Any attraction he might feel for her was irrelevant. He had testimony to give and a corruption case to solve, and the job always came first.

Carlson's email had come late this morning, so Tom hadn't had time to do his research. That was the only reason Judge Jennings had caught him off guard.

Because Judge Jennings was at least twenty years younger than he had anticipated. Everyone else who had sat on that bench had tended to be white, male and well north of fifty years old.

Maybe that was why she seemed so young, although she was no teenager. She was probably in her thirties, Tom guessed. She had light brown hair that was pulled back into a low ponytail—but it wasn't severely scraped away from her face. Instead, her hair looked like it had a natural wave and she let it frame her features, softening the lines of her sharp cheekbones. She wore a simple pair of stud earrings—diamonds or reasonable fakes, he noticed when she turned her head and they caught the light. Her makeup was understated and professional, and she wore a lace collar on top of her black robe.

She was, he realized, *beautiful*. Which was an interesting observation on his part.

He had no problems noting the physical beauty of

men or women. For Tom, the last ten years had been one long observation of the human condition. Looking at an attractive person was like studying fine art. Even if a woman's physical attributes didn't move him, he could still appreciate her beauty.

But his visceral reaction to a woman in shapeless judge's robes was not some cerebral observation of conventional beauty. It was a punch to the gut. When was the last time he'd felt that unmistakable spark?

Well, he knew the answer to that. But he wouldn't let thoughts of Stephanie break free of the box in which he kept them locked up tight. He wouldn't think about it now. Maybe not ever.

He sat back and did what he did best—he watched and waited. Judge Caroline Jennings ran an efficient courtroom. When Lasky, the defense lawyer, started to grandstand, she cut him off. She wasn't confrontational, but she wasn't cowed by anyone.

As he waited for his name to be called, Tom mentally ran back through the email Carlson had sent him. Caroline Jennings was an outsider, appointed to fill the seat on the bench left vacant after Tom had arrested the last judge.

She was from Minneapolis—which was a hell of a long way from South Dakota. In theory, she had no connection with local politics—or lobbyists. That didn't mean she was clean. Whoever was pulling the strings in the state would be interested in making friends with the new judge.

Once, Tom would've been encouraged by the fact that she had already contacted Carlson about an unusual flower delivery. Surely, the reasoning went, if she was already willing to identify such gifts as suspicious, she was an honest person.

Tom wasn't that naive anymore. He didn't know who was buying off judges, although he had a few guesses. He couldn't prove his suspicions one way or the other. But he did know that whatever group—or groups—was rigging the courts in his home state, they played deep. He wouldn't put it past anyone in this scenario to offer up a beautiful, fresh-faced young judge as a mole—or a distraction.

"The prosecution calls FBI Special Agent Thomas Yellow Bird to the stand."

Tom snapped to attention, standing and straightening his tie. He should've been paying more attention to the trial at hand than musing about the new judge. The prosecutor had warned him that this particular defense lawyer liked to put members of law enforcement on the spot.

As he moved to the front of the room, he could feel Judge Jennings's gaze upon him. He didn't allow himself to look back. He kept his meanest gaze trained on the accused, enjoying the way the moron shrank back behind his lawyer. It didn't matter how intriguing—yes, that was the right word. It didn't matter how *intriguing* Judge Caroline Jennings was—Tom had to see justice served on the man who'd pulled a gun on a bank teller and made off with seven thousand dollars and change.

All the same, Tom wanted to look at her. Would she still have that challenge on her face? Or would he see suspicion? He was used to that. He'd been called inscrutable on more than one occasion—and that was by people who knew him. Tom had a hell of a poker face, which was an asset in his line of work. People couldn't figure him out, and they chose to interpret their confusion as distrust.

Or would he see something else in her eyes—the same pull he'd felt when she'd walked into this courtroom? Would she still have that delicate blush?

Smith, the prosecutor, caught Tom's eye and gave him a look. Right. Tom had a job to do before he dug into the mystery that was Caroline Jennings.

Leland swore Tom in, and he took his seat on the witness stand. Roses, he thought, not allowing himself to look in her direction. She smelled like roses, lush and in full bloom.

Smith, in a forgettable brown suit that matched his equally forgettable name, asked Tom all the usual questions—how he had been brought in on the case, where the leads had taken the investigation, how he had determined that the accused was guilty of the crime, how the arrest had gone down, what the accused had said during questioning.

It was cut-and-dried, really. He had to keep from yawning.

Satisfied, Smith said, "Your witness," and returned to his seat.

The defense lawyer didn't do anything for a moment. He continued to sit at his table, reviewing his notes. This was a tactic Tom had seen countless times, and he wasn't about to let the man unnerve him. He waited. Patiently.

"Counsel, your witness," Judge Jennings said, an edge in her voice. Tom almost smiled at that. She was not as patient as she'd seemed.

Then the defense lawyer stood. He took his time organizing his space, taking a drink—every piddling little thing a lawyer could do to stall.

"Today, Counselor," Judge Jennings snapped.

She got a lawyer's smile for that one before Lasky said, "Of course, Your Honor. Agent Yellow Bird, where were you on the evening of April twenty-seventh, the day you were supposedly tracing the bills stolen from the American State Bank of Pierre?"

The way he said it—drawing out the *Yellow Bird* part and hitting the *supposedly* with extra punch—did nothing to improve Tom's opinion of the man. If this guy was trying to make Tom's Lakota heritage an issue, he was in for a rude awakening.

Still, Tom was under oath and he responded, "I was off duty," in a level voice. This wasn't his first time on the stand. He knew how this gotcha game was played, and he wasn't going to give this jerk anything to build off.

"Doing what?" That smile again.

Tom let the question linger in the air just long enough. Smith roused out of his stunned stupor and shouted, "Objection, Your Honor! What Agent Yellow Bird does in his free time is of no importance to this court."

The defense attorney turned his attention to the judge, that oily smile at full power. "Your Honor, I intend to show that what Agent Yellow Bird does on his own time directly compromises his ability to do his job."

What a load of bull. That perp was guilty of robbing a bank, and his defense team was throwing everything and the kitchen sink at the prosecutor's witnesses in an effort to throw the trial. Tom knew it, the prosecutor knew it and the defense attorney definitely knew it.

But none of that mattered. All that mattered was the opinion of Judge Caroline Jennings. She cleared her throat, which made Tom look at her. Then she leaned forward, elbows on her desk. "How so, Counselor?"

"Your Honor?"

"You're obviously building toward something. My time is valuable—as is yours, I assume. Someone's paying the bills, right?"

It took everything Tom had not to burst out laughing at that—but he kept all facial muscles on complete lockdown.

The defense lawyer tried to smile, but Tom could tell the man was losing his grip. Clearly, he'd expected Judge Jennings to be an easy mark. "If I could ask the question, I'd be able to demonstrate—"

"Because it sounds like you're fishing," Judge Jennings interrupted. "What illegal activity are you going to accuse Agent Yellow Bird of?" She turned her attention to Tom and there it was again—that *pull*. "Any crimes you'd like to admit to, just to save us all the time?"

Tom notched an eyebrow at her, unable to keep his

lips from twitching. "Your Honor, the only crime I'm guilty of is occasionally driving too fast."

Something changed in her eyes—deepened. He hoped like hell it was appreciation. All he knew was that he appreciated that look. "Yes," she murmured, her soft voice pouring oil on the fire that was racing through his body. "South Dakota seems made for speeding."

Oh, hell, yeah—he'd like to gun his engine and let it run right about now.

She turned her attention back to the attorney. "Are you going to make the argument that violating speed limits compromises an FBI agent's ability to investigate a crime?"

"Prostitutes!" the flustered lawyer yelled, waving a manila envelope around in the air. "He patronizes *prostitutes*!"

An absolute hush fell over the courtroom—which was saying something, as it hadn't been loud to begin with.

Shit. How had this slimeball found out about *that*?

"Your Honor!" Smith shot out of his chair, moving with more animation than Tom would have given him credit for. "That has nothing to do with a bank robbery!"

This was ridiculous, but Tom knew how this game was played. If he displayed irritation or looked nervous, it'd make him look shifty—which was exactly what the defense wanted. So he did—and said—nothing. Not a damn thing.

But his jaw flexed. He was not ashamed of his after-hours activities, but if Judge Jennings let this line of questioning go on, it could compromise some of his girls—and those girls had been compromised enough.

"That's a serious accusation," Judge Jennings said in a voice that was so cold it dropped the temperature in the courtroom a whole ten degrees. "I assume you have proof?"

"Proof?" the lawyer repeated and waved the manila envelope in the air. "Of course I have proof. I wouldn't waste the court's valuable time if I couldn't back it up."

"Let me see."

The defense lawyer paused—which proved to be his undoing.

Judge Jennings narrowed her gaze and said, "Counselor Lasky, if you have evidence that Agent Yellow Bird patronizes prostitutes—*and* that somehow compromises his ability to trace stolen bills—I'd suggest you produce it within the next five seconds or I will hold you in contempt of this court. Care to start a tab at five hundred dollars?"

Not that Tom would admit this in a court of law, but Caroline Jennings had just taken that spark of attraction and fanned it into a full-fledged flame of desire, because the woman was amazing. Simply *amazing.*

Lasky only hesitated for a second before he strode forward and handed the manila envelope over to Judge Jennings. She pulled out what looked to be some grainy photos. Tom guessed they'd been pulled from a security camera, but at this angle he couldn't see who was in the pictures or where they might have been taken.

He knew what they weren't pictures of—him in flagrante delicto with hookers. Having dinner with hookers, maybe. He did that all the time. But last he checked, buying a girl dinner wasn't illegal.

Even so, that the defense lawyer had the pictures was not good. Tom had a responsibility to those girls and his tribe. But more than that, he had an obligation to the FBI to make sure that what he did when he was off the clock didn't compromise the pursuit of justice. And if Judge Jennings let this line of questioning go on, Tom's time at the truck stops would be fair game for every single defense attorney in the state. Hell, even if this criminal wasn't found guilty, another defense lawyer would try the same line of attack, hoping to be more successful.

"Your Honor," Smith finally piped up into the silence, "this entire line of questioning is irrelevant to the case at hand. For all the court knows, he was meeting with informants!"

Not helping, Tom thought darkly, although again, he didn't react. If people suspected those girls were turning informant, they'd be in even more danger.

Judge Jennings ignored Smith. "Mr. Lasky, as far as I can tell, this is proof that Agent Yellow Bird eats meals with other people."

"Who are known prostitutes!" Lasky crowed, aiming for conviction but nailing desperation instead.

Smith started to object again, but Judge Jennings raised a hand to cut him off. "That's it? That's all you've got? He ate—" She turned to face Tom and held out a photo. "Is this dinner or lunch?"

Tom recognized the Crossroads Truck Stop immediately—that was Jeannie. "Dinner."

"He ate dinner with a woman? Did she launder the stolen money? Drive the getaway car? Was she the inside woman?"

"Well—no," Lasky sputtered. "She doesn't have anything to do with this case!" The second the words left his mouth, he realized what he'd said, and his entire face crumpled in defeat.

"You've got that right." Amazingly, Judge Jennings sounded more disappointed than anything else, as if she'd expected Lasky to put up a better fight. "Anything else you have to add?"

Lasky slumped and shook his head.

"Your Honor," Smith said, relief all over his face, "move to strike the defense's comments from the record."

"Granted." She fixed a steely gaze on Lasky.

Tom realized he'd never seen such a woman as Judge Jennings—especially not one for whom he'd felt that spark. He wanted nothing more than to chase that fire, keep fanning those flames. Stephanie would have wanted him to move on—he knew that. But no one else had ever caught his attention like this, and he wasn't going to settle for anything less than everything. So he'd stayed faithful to his late wife and focused on his job.

Except for now. Except for Caroline Jennings.

There was one problem with this unreasonable attraction.

She was his next assignment. Damn it.

"Agent Yellow Bird, you may step down," she said to him.

Tom made damn sure to keep his movements calm and even. He didn't gloat and he didn't strut. Looking like he'd gotten away with something would undermine his position of authority, so he stood straight and tall and, without sparing a glance for the defense attorney or his client, Tom walked out of the courtroom.

There. His work on the bank robbery case was done. Which meant one thing and one thing only.

Caroline Jennings was now his sole focus.

He was looking forward to this.

Two

As Caroline headed out into the oppressive South Dakota heat at the end of the day, she knew she should be thinking about who had sent the flowers. Or about James Carlson's brief reply to her email saying he had contacted an associate, who would be in touch. She should be thinking about the day's cases. Or tomorrow's cases.

At the very least, she should be thinking about what she was going to eat for dinner. She had been relying heavily on carryout for the last couple of months, because she hadn't finished unpacking yet. She should be formulating her plan of attack to get the remaining boxes emptied so she could have a fully functional kitchen again by this weekend at the latest and make better food choices.

She wasn't thinking about any of those things. Instead, all she could think about was a certain FBI agent with incredible eyes.

Thomas Yellow Bird. She shivered just thinking of the way his gaze had connected with hers across the courtroom. Even at that distance, she'd felt the heat behind his gaze. Oh, he was intense. The way he'd kept his cool under fire when that defense attorney had gone after him? The way he'd glared at the accused? Hell, the way he'd let the corner of his mouth twitch into a smile that had threatened to melt her faster than ice cream on a summer day when he'd said he was guilty of speeding?

So dangerous. Because if he could have this sort of effect on her with just a look, what would he be capable of with his hands—or without an audience?

She hadn't had the time or inclination to investigate the dating scene in the greater Pierre area. She assumed the pool of eligible men would be considerably smaller than it was in Minneapolis—not that she'd dated a lot back home. It'd been low on her priority list, both there and here. Messy relationships were just that—messy. Dating—and sex—left too much room for mistakes, the kind she'd dodged once already.

No, thank you. She did not need to slip up and get tied to a man she wasn't even sure she wanted to marry. Her career was far more important than that.

Besides, she spent most of her time with lawyers and alleged criminals. Her bailiff was married. It wasn't like an attractive, intelligent man she could date without a conflict of professional interest just showed up in her courtroom every day.

Except for today. Maybe.

Because there was that small matter of whether or not he patronized prostitutes. That was a deal breaker.

Lost in thought, she rounded the corner of the courthouse and pulled up short. Because an attractive, intelligent man—FBI Special Agent Thomas Yellow Bird—was leaning on a sleek muscle car parked two slots down from her Volvo. Her nipples tightened immediately, and only one thing could soothe them.

Him.

She shook that thought right out of her head. Good Lord, a man shouldn't look this sinful—and in those sunglasses? He was every bad-boy fantasy come to life. But she'd watched him on the stand and seen flashes of humor underneath his intense looks and stoic expressions—and that? *That* was what made him truly sexy.

Was secretly lusting after an FBI agent in a great suit a conflict of interest? God, she hoped not. Because that suit was amazing on him.

"Agent Yellow Bird," she said when he straightened. "This is a surprise."

One corner of his mouth kicked up as he pulled his sunglasses off. "Not a bad one, I hope."

It wasn't like they'd had a personal conversation in court today. There'd been several feet of plywood between them. She'd been wearing her robes. Everything had been mediated through Lasky and Smith. Cheryl had recorded every word.

Here? None of those barriers existed.

"That depends," she answered honestly. Because if he were going to ask her out, it could be a very good thing. But if this was about something else… then maybe not so much.

His gaze drifted over her, a leisurely appraisal that did nothing for Caroline's peace of mind right now. She'd thought she'd been imagining that appraisal in the courtroom when she'd met his gaze across the crowded courtroom and everything about her—her clothes, her skin—had suddenly felt too tight and too loose at the same time.

No, no—not lusting after him. Lust was a weakness and weakness was a risk. The heat flooding her body had more to do with the July sun than this man.

As his gaze made its way back up to her face, a look of appreciation plain to see, she knew she wasn't imagining *this*. When he spoke, it was almost a relief. "I wanted to thank you for having my back today."

She waved away this statement, glad to have something to focus on other than his piercing eyes. "Just doing my job. Last time I checked, eating dinner wasn't a conflict of interest." Unlike this conversation. Maybe. "I have no desire in being perceived as weak on the bench. I run a tight ship."

"So I noticed."

This would be a wonderful time for him to assure her that he didn't patronize prostitutes—in fact, it'd be great if he didn't eat dinner with them at all. She tried to keep in mind what Smith had said in his objections—perhaps Agent Yellow Bird had been meeting with informants or some other reasonable explanation that could be tied directly to his job.

Strangely, she wasn't feeling reasonable about Agent Yellow Bird right now. She steeled her resolve. She couldn't be swayed by a gorgeous man in a great suit any more than she could be influenced by cut flowers. Not even loyalty could corrupt her. Not anymore.

Everything about him—his gaze, his manner—was intense. And, at least right now, they were on the same side. She'd hate to be a criminal in his sights.

"Well," she said, feeling awkward about this whole encounter.

"Well," he agreed. He shoved off his car—an aggressive-looking black thing with a silver stripe on the hood that screamed *power*—and extended his hand. His suit jacket shifted, and she caught a glimpse of his gun. "We haven't been formally introduced. I'm Tom Yellow Bird."

"Tom." She hesitated before slipping her palm into his. This didn't count as a conflict of interest, right? Of course not. This was merely a...professional courtesy. Yes, that was it. "Caroline Jennings."

That got her a real smile—one that took him from intensely handsome to devastatingly so. Her knees weakened—weakened, for God's sake! It only got worse when he said, "Caroline," in a voice that was closer to reverence than respectability as his fingers closed around hers.

A rush of what felt like electricity passed from where her skin met his, so powerful that Caroline jolted. Images flashed through her mind of him pulling her in closer, his mouth covering hers, his hands covering…

"Sorry," she said, pulling her hand back. She knew she was blushing fiercely, but she was going to blame that on the heat. "I generate a lot of static electricity." Which was true. In the winter, when the air was dry and she was walking on carpeting.

It was at least ninety-four out today, with humidity she could swim in. She was so hot that sweat was beginning to trickle down her back.

He notched an eyebrow at her, and she got the feeling he was laughing. But definitely on the inside, because his mouth didn't move from that cocky half grin.

Her breasts ached, and she didn't think she could blame that on the sun. She was flushed and desperately needed to get the hell out of her skirt suit to cool down. What she wouldn't give for a swim in a cool pool right now.

Alone. Definitely alone. Not with Agent Tom Yellow Bird. Nope.

"About the flowers," Tom said, looking almost regretful about bringing up the subject as he leaned back against his spotless car.

Caroline recoiled. "What?" It wasn't as if the fact that she'd received the bouquet wasn't common knowledge—it was. Everyone in the courthouse knew, thanks to Andrea passing out roses to anyone who'd take some. Leland had taken a huge bunch home for his wife. Even Cheryl had taken a few, favoring Caroline with a rare smile. Caroline had left the remaining few blooms in her office. She didn't want them in her house.

Had Agent Yellow Bird sent them? Was this whole conversation—the intense looks, the cocky grins—because he was trying to butter her up?

Crap, what if Lasky had been right? What if Agent Tom Yellow Bird was crooked and prostitutes were just the tip of the iceberg?

Suddenly her blood was running cold. She moved to step past him. "The flowers were lovely. But I'm not interested."

Damn, she was tough.

"Whoa," Tom said, holding his hands up in the universal sign of surrender. "I didn't send them."

"I'm sure," Caroline murmured, stepping around him and heading for her car as if he suddenly smelled.

"Caroline," he said again, and damn if it didn't come out with a note of tenderness. Which was ridiculous. He had no reason to feel tender toward her at all. She was his assignment, whether she liked it or not. It'd be easier if she cooperated, of course, but he'd get to the bottom of things one way or the other.

He was nothing if not patient.

She began to walk faster. "I appreciate the gesture, but I'm not interested. I hold myself to a higher standard of ethics and integrity."

What the hell? Clearly, she thought he'd sent the flowers. The idea was so comical he almost laughed. "Wait." He fell in step beside her. "Carlson sent me."

"Did he?" She didn't stop.

He dug his phone out of his pocket. If she wouldn't believe him, maybe she'd believe Carlson. "Here." Just as she made it to her car, he shoved his phone in front of her face. She had to stop to keep from slamming her nose into the screen. "See?"

She shot him an irritated look—which made him smile. She was tough—but he was tougher.

Begrudgingly, she read Carlson's email out loud. "'Tom—the new judge, Caroline Jennings, contacted me. An anonymous person sent her flowers and apparently that's out of the ordinary for her. See what you can find out. If we're lucky, this will open the case back up. Maggie sends her love. Carlson.'"

She frowned as she read it. This was as close as Tom had been to her and again, he was surrounded by the perfume of roses. He wanted to lean in close and press his lips against the base of her neck to see if she tasted as sweet as she smelled—but if he'd gauged Caroline Jennings right, she probably had Mace on her keys. Given the way she was holding her body, he'd bet she'd taken some self-defense classes at some point.

Good for her. He liked a woman who wasn't afraid to defend herself.

The moment that thought popped up, Tom slammed the door on it. He didn't like Judge Jennings, no matter how sweet she smelled or how strongly he felt that pull. This was about the case. The job was all he had.

She angled her body toward his, and a primal part of his brain crowed in satisfaction when she didn't step back. If anything, it felt like she was challenging his space with her body. “And I’m supposed to believe that’s on the level, huh?”

God, he’d like to be challenged. She was simply magnificent—even better out of her robes. “I don’t play games, Caroline,” he said. No matter how much he might want to. “Not about something like this.”

She studied him for a moment. “That implies you play games in other situations, though.”

His lips twisted to one side and he crossed his arms, because if he didn’t, he might start smiling and that was bad for his image as a no-holds-barred lawman. “That all depends on the game, doesn’t it?”

“I put more stock in the players.”

So much for his image, because he burst out laughing at that. Caroline took a step back, her hands clenched at her sides and her back ramrod straight—which was completely at odds with the unexpectedly intense look of…longing? She looked less like a woman about to punch him and more like…

Like she was holding herself back. Like she wanted to laugh with him. Maybe do even more with him.

If he slid an arm around her waist and pulled her into his chest, would she break his nose or would she go all soft and womanly against him? How long had it been since he’d had a woman in his arms?

It absolutely did not matter—nor did it matter that he knew exactly how long it’d been. What mattered was cracking this case.

“I don’t sleep with them.”

"What?" She physically recoiled, pushing herself closer to the door.

"The prostitutes," he explained. "I don't sleep with them. That's what you're worried about, isn't it? What I do in my free time?"

"It's none of my business what you do when you're off duty," she said in a stiff voice, shrinking even farther away from him. "It's a free country."

That made him grin again. "This country is bought and paid for, and you and I both know it," he said, surprised at the bitterness that sneaked in there. "I buy them dinner," he went on, wondering if someone like Caroline Jennings would ever really be able to understand. "They're mostly young, mostly girls—mostly being forced to work against their will. I treat them like people, not criminals—show them there's another way. When they're ready, I help them get away and get clean. And until they are, I make sure they're eating, give them enough money they don't have to work that night."

"That's…" She blinked. *"Really?"*

"Really. I don't sleep with them." For some ridiculous reason, he almost let the truth slip free—he didn't sleep with anyone. It was none of her business—but he wanted to make sure she knew he operated with all the ethical integrity she valued. "Carlson can back me up on that."

"Who's Maggie?"

Interesting. There was no good reason for her to be concerned about Maggie sending Tom her love, unless…

Unless Caroline was trying to figure out if he was attached. "Carlson's wife. We grew up on the same reservation together." He left out the part where he'd gone off to Washington, DC, and joined the FBI, leaving Maggie vulnerable to exploitation and abuse.

There was a reason he didn't sleep with prostitutes. But that wasn't his story to tell—it was Maggie's. He stuck to the facts.

The breeze gusted, surrounding him with her scent. He couldn't help leaning forward and inhaling. "Roses," he murmured, his voice unexpectedly tender again. He really needed to stop with the tenderness.

She flushed again, and although he shouldn't, he hoped it wasn't from the heat. "I beg your pardon?"

"You smell of roses." Somehow, he managed to put another step between them. "Is that your normal perfume, or was that from the delivery?" There. That was a perfectly reasonable question to ask, from a law-enforcement perspective.

"From the flowers. The bouquet was huge. At least a hundred stems."

"All roses?"

She thought about that. "Mixed. Lilies and carnations—a little bit of everything, really. But mostly roses."

In other words, it hadn't been cheap. He tried to visualize how big a vase with a hundred stems would be. "But you're not taking any home with you?"

She shook her head. "I didn't want them. My clerk got rid of most of them. Leland took home a huge bunch for his wife."

"Leland's a good guy," Tom replied, as if this were normal small talk when it was anything but.

"How do I know I can trust you?" she blurted out.

"My record speaks for itself." He pulled a business card out of his pocket and held it out to her. "You don't know what you're up against here. This kind of corruption is insidious and nearly impossible to track, Caroline. But if there's anything else out of the ordinary—and I mean *anything*—don't hesitate to call me. Or Carlson," he added, almost as an afterthought. He didn't want her to call Carlson, though. He wanted her to call him. For any reason. "No detail is too small. Names, car makes—anything you remember can be helpful."

After a long moment—so long, in fact, that he began to wonder if she was going to take the card at all—she asked, "So we're to work together?"

He heard the question she didn't ask. "On this case, yes."

But if it weren't for this case…

She took the card from him and slid it into her shirt pocket. He did his best not to stare at the motion. *Damn.*

She gave him that look again, the one that made him think she was holding herself back. "Fine."

He straightened and gave her a little salute. "After this case…" He turned and headed to his car. "Have a good evening, Caroline," he called over his shoulder.

She gasped and he almost, *almost* spun back on his heel and captured that little noise with a kiss.

But he didn't. Instead, he climbed into the driver's

seat of his Camaro, gunned the engine and peeled out of the parking lot as fast as he could.

He needed to put a lot of distance between him and Caroline Jennings. Because, no matter how much he might be attracted to her, he wasn't about to compromise this case for her.

And that was final.

Three

For a while, nothing happened. There were no more mysterious flower deliveries—or, for that matter, any kind of deliveries. The remaining half dozen roses on Caroline's desk withered and died. Andrea threw them away. People in the courthouse seemed friendlier—apparently, handing out scads of flowers made Caroline quite popular. Other than that, though, things continued on as they had before.

Before Agent Tom Yellow Bird had shown up in her courtroom.

She got up, went for a jog before the heat got oppressive, went to the courthouse and then came home. No mysterious gifts, no handsome men—mysterious or otherwise. No surprises. Everything went exactly as it was supposed to. Which was good. Great, even.

If she didn't have Tom's card in her pocket—and that electric memory of shaking his hand—she would have been tempted to convince herself she had imagined the whole thing. A fantasy she'd invented to alleviate boredom instead of a flesh-and-blood man. Fantasies were always safer, anyway.

But...there were times when she could almost feel his presence. She'd come out of the courthouse and pull up short, looking for his black muscle car with the silver stripe on the hood, but he was never there. And the fact that disappointed her was irritating.

She had not developed a crush on the man. No crushes. That was that.

Just because he was an officer of the law with a gun concealed under his jacket, with eyes that might be his biggest weapon—that was no reason to lust after the man. She didn't need to see him again. It was better that way—at least, she finally had to admit to herself, it was better that way while his corruption investigation was still ongoing. The more distance between them, the less she would become infatuated.

Tom Yellow Bird was a mistake she wasn't going to make.

It was a good theory, anyway. But he showed up in her dreams, a shadowy lover who drove her wild with his hands, his mouth, his body. She woke up tense and frustrated, and no electronic assistance could relieve the pressure. Her vibrator barely took the edge off, but it was enough.

Besides, she had other things to focus on. She finally finished unpacking her kitchen, although she still ate too much takeout. It was hard to work up the energy to cook when the temperature outside kept pushing a hundred.

Still, she tried. She came home one Friday after work three weeks after the floral delivery, juggling a couple of bags of groceries. Eggs were on sale and there was a recipe for summery quiche on Pinterest that she wanted to try. She had air-conditioning and a weekend to kick back. She was going to cook—or else. At the very least, she was going to eat ice cream.

She knew the moment she unlocked the front door that something was wrong. She couldn't have said what it was because, when she looked around the living room, nothing seemed out of place. But there was an overwhelming sense that someone had been in her home that she didn't dare ignore.

Heart pounding, she backed out of the house, pulling the door shut behind her. She carried the groceries right back out to the trunk of her car and then, hands shaking, she pulled her cell phone and Tom's card out of her pocket and dialed.

He answered on the second ring. "Yes?"

"Is this Agent Yellow Bird?" He sounded gruffer on the phone—so gruff, in fact, that she couldn't be sure it was the same man who had laughed with her in the parking lot.

"Caroline? Are you all right?"

Suddenly, she felt silly. She was sitting outside in the car. It wasn't like the door had been jimmied open. It hadn't even looked like anything had been moved—at least, not in the living room. "It's probably nothing."

"I'll be the judge of that. What's going on?"

She exhaled in relief. She was not a damsel in distress and she did not need a white knight to come riding to her rescue. But there was something comforting about the thought that a federal agent was ready and willing to take over if things weren't on the up and up. "I just got home and it feels like there was someone in my house." She winced. It didn't sound any less silly when she said it out loud.

There was a moment of silence on the other end of the phone, and she got a sinking feeling that he was going to tell her not to be such a ninny. "Where are you?"

"In my car. In the driveway," she added. Cars could be anywhere.

"If you're comfortable, stay there. I'm about fifteen minutes away. If you aren't, I want you to leave and drive someplace safe. Understand?"

"Okay." His words should have been reassuring. He was on his way over and she had a plan. But, perversely, the fact that he was taking this feeling so seriously scared her even more.

What if someone really had been in her house? It hadn't looked like a robbery. What had they been after?

"Call me back if you need to. I'm on my way." Before she could even respond, he hung up.

Wait, she thought, staring at the screen of her phone—how did he know where she lived?

She turned on her car—all the better to make a quick getaway—and cranked the AC. She knew she shouldn't have bought ice cream at the store, but too late now.

She waited and watched her house. Nothing happened. No one slunk out. Not so much as a curtain twitched. It looked perfectly normal, and by the time Tom came roaring down the street, she had convinced herself she was being ridiculous. She got out of the car again and went to meet him.

"I'm sorry to bother you," she began. "I'm sure it's nothing."

Then she pulled up short. Gone was the slick custom-made suit. Instead, a pair of well-worn jeans hung low off his hips and a soft white T-shirt clung to his chest. He had his shoulder holster on, which only highlighted his pecs all the more. Her mouth went dry as his long legs powerfully closed the distance between them.

If she had been daydreaming about Agent Yellow Bird in a suit, the man in a pair of blue jeans was going to haunt her dreams in the very best way possible.

He walked right up to her and put his hands on her shoulders. "Are you all right?" he asked, his voice low.

That spark of electricity moved over her skin again, and she shivered. "Fine," she said, but her voice wavered. "I'm not sure I can say the same for the ice cream, but life will go on."

He almost smiled. She could tell, because his eyes

crinkled ever so slightly. "Why do you think someone was in your house?" As he spoke, his hands drifted down her shoulders until he was holding her upper arms. A good two feet of space still separated them, but it was almost an embrace.

At least, that's how it felt to her. But what did she know? She couldn't even tell if someone had been in her house or not.

"It was just a feeling. The door wasn't busted, and nothing seemed out of place in the living room." She tried to laugh it off, but she didn't even manage to convince herself.

He squeezed her arms before dropping his hands. She felt oddly lost without his touch. "Is the door still unlocked?" She nodded. "Stay behind me." He pulled his gun and moved forward. Caroline stayed close. "Quietly," he added as he opened the door.

Silently, they entered the house. Her skin crawled and she unconsciously hooked her hand into the waistband of his jeans. Tom checked each room, but there was no one there. Caroline looked at everything, but nothing seemed out of place. By the time they peeked into the unused guest room, with the remaining boxes from the move still haphazardly stacked, she felt more than silly. She felt stupid.

When Tom holstered his gun and turned to face her, she knew her cheeks were flaming red. "I'm sorry, I—"

They were standing very close together in the hall, and Tom reached out and touched a finger to her lips.

Then he stepped in closer and whispered in her ear, "Outside."

For a second, neither of them moved. She could feel the heat of his body, and she had an almost overwhelming urge to kiss the finger resting against her lips. Which was ridiculous.

What was it about this man that turned her into a blubbering schoolgirl with a crush? Maybe she was just trying to bury her embarrassment at having called him out here for nothing beneath a more manageable emotion—lust. Not that lust was a bad thing. Except for the fact that she still had no idea what he did in his spare time or whether or not it broke any laws. And there was the unavoidable fact that acting on any lust would be a conflict of interest.

They were actively on an investigation, for crying out loud. It was one of the reasons she couldn't read romantic suspense novels—it drove her nuts when people in the middle of a dangerous situation dropped everything to get naked.

She was not that kind of girl, damn it. So instead of leaning into his touch or wrapping her arms around his waist and pulling him in tight, she did the right thing. She nodded and pulled away.

It was harder than she'd thought it would be.

When they were outside, she tried apologizing again. "I'm so sorry that I called you out here for nothing." She didn't enjoy making a fool of herself, but when it happened, she tried to own up to the mistake as quickly as possible.

He leaned against her car, studying her. She had

met a lot of hard-nosed investigators and steely-eyed lawyers in her time, but nothing quite compared to Tom Yellow Bird. "Are you sure it was nothing? Tell me again how you felt there was something wrong."

She shrugged helplessly. "It was just a feeling. Everything looked fine, and you saw yourself that there was no one in the house." She decided that worse than feeling stupid was the fact that she had made herself look weak.

For some ridiculous reason, this situation reminded her of her brother. Trent Jennings had been a master of creating a crisis where none existed—and he was even better at making it seem like it was her fault. Because she'd been the mistake, the squalling brat who'd taken his parents away from him. Or so he was fond of reminding her.

That wasn't what she was doing here, was it? Creating a crisis in order to focus the attention on herself? No, she didn't think so. The house had *felt* wrong. Then something occurred to her. "Why are we outside again? It's hot out here."

"The place is probably bugged."

He said it so casually that it took a few moments before his words actually sank in. *"What?"*

"I've seen this before."

"I don't understand," she said, wondering if he was ever going to answer a straight question. "You've seen *what* before?"

For a moment, he looked miserable—the face of a man who was about to deliver bad news. "You have a feeling that someone was in your house—although nothing appears to have been moved or taken, correct?"

She nodded. "So my sixth sense is having a bad day. How does that mean there are bugs in my house?"

One corner of his mouth crept up. "They're trying to find something they can use against you. Maybe you have some sort of peccadillo or kink, maybe something from your past." He smiled, but it wasn't reassuring. "Something worse than speeding tickets?"

The blood drained from her face. She didn't have any kinks, definitely nothing that would be incriminating. She didn't want people to watch when she used her vibrator—the thought was horrifying. But...

It would be embarrassing if people found out about her lapse of judgment in college. Although, since her parents were dead, she wouldn't have to face their disappointment, and the odds of Trent finding out about it were slim, since they didn't talk anymore.

But more than that...what if people connected her back to Vincent Verango? That wouldn't just be embarrassing. That had the potential of being career ending. Would she never be able to escape the legacy of the Verango case?

No, this was fine. Panicking would be a mistake right now. She needed to keep her calm. "I stay within five miles of the speed limit," she said, trying to arrange her face into something that wasn't incriminating.

Tom shrugged. At least he was interpreting her reaction as shock and not guilt. "They want something on you so that when they approach you again and you say you're not interested, they'll have a threat with teeth. If you don't want them to inform the Justice Department about this embarrassing or illegal thing, you'll do what they say. Simple."

"Simple?" She gaped at him, wondering when the world had stopped making sense. "Nothing about that is simple!"

"I don't have a bug detector," he went on, as if she hadn't spoken. "And seeing as it's Friday night, I don't think I can get one before Monday."

"Why not?" Because she couldn't imagine this oh-so-simple situation didn't justify a damned bug detector.

A muscle in his jaw twitched. "I'm off duty for the next four days. I'd have to make a special case to get one, and Carlson and I like to keep our investigations off the record as much as possible."

She couldn't help it—she laughed. She sounded horrible, even to her own ears, but it was either that or cry. This entire situation was so far beyond the realm of normal that she briefly considered she might've fallen asleep in her office this afternoon.

"The way I see it," he went on, again ignoring her outburst, "you have two choices. You can go about your business as normal and I'll come back on Monday and sweep the house."

It was, hands-down, the most reasonable suggestion she was probably going to hear. So why did it make her stomach turn with an anxious sort of dread? "Okay. What's my other choice?"

That muscle in his jaw ticked again, and she realized that he looked hard—like a stone, no emotions at all. The playful grin was nowhere to be seen. "You come with me."

"Like, to your home?" That was it. She was definitely dreaming. It wasn't like her to nod off in her chambers, but what other reasonable explanation was there?

"In a professional capacity," he said in what was probably supposed to be a reassuring tone.

Caroline was not reassured. "If they bugged my house and I'm new here, why would your home be any less susceptible to surveillance?"

And just like that, his stony expression was gone. He cracked a grin and again, she thought of a wolf—dangerous but playful. And she had no idea if she was the prey or not.

"Trust me," he said, pushing off the car and coming to stand directly in front of her. "Nothing gets past me."

Four

They had been in the car for an hour and fifteen minutes. Seventy-five *silent* minutes. Any attempt at conversation was met with—at best—a grunt. Mostly, Tom just ignored her, so she stopped trying.

Pierre was a distant memory and Tom was, true to his word, breaking every speed limit known to mankind and the state of South Dakota. She'd be willing to bet they were topping out well past one hundred, so she chose not to look at the speedometer, lest she start thinking of fiery crashes along the side of the road.

There was no avoiding Tom Yellow Bird. This muscle car was aggressive—just like him. He filled the driver's seat effortlessly, seemingly becoming one with his machine. She didn't know much about cars, but she could tell this was a nice one. The seats were a supple leather and the dashboard had all sorts of connected gadgets that were a mystery to her.

Just like the man next to her.

The landscape outside the car hadn't changed since they'd hit the open plains, so she turned her attention to Tom. They were driving west and he still had his sunglasses on. She couldn't read him. The only thing that gave her a clue to his mental state was how he kept tapping his fingers on the steering wheel. At least, she thought it was a clue. He might just be bored out of his mind.

It wasn't fair. She hadn't thought of the Verango case in, what—ten years? Twelve? But that was exactly the sort of thing a bad guy would be looking for, because she didn't have anything kinky hiding in her closet. And a vibrator didn't count. At least she hoped it didn't.

She liked sex. She'd like to have more of it, preferably with someone like Tom—but only if it were the kind that couldn't come back to bite her. No messy relationships, no birth control slipups, no strings attached.

Not that she wanted to have sex with *him*. But the man had inspired weeks of wet dreams, all because he had an intense look and an air of invulnerability about him. And that body. Who could forget that body?

She wished like hell she didn't have this primal reaction to him. Even riding next to him was torture. She was aware of him in a way she couldn't ignore, no matter how hard she tried. She felt it when he shifted in his seat, as if there were invisible threads binding them together. And that wasn't even the worst of it. Although he had the AC blasting on high, she was the kind of hot that had nothing to do with the temperature outside. Her bra was too tight and she wanted out of this top.

She'd love to go for a swim. She needed to do something to cool down before she did something ridiculous, like parading around his home in nothing but her panties.

And the fact that her brain was even suggesting that as a viable way to kill a weekend was a freaking *huge* problem. Because getting naked anywhere near Tom Yellow Bird would be a mistake. Yes, it might very well be a mistake she enjoyed making—but that wouldn't change the fact that it would still be a gross error in judgment, one that might compromise a case or—worse—get her blackmailed. A mistake like that could derail her entire career—and for what? For a man who wasn't even talking to her? No. She couldn't make another mistake like that.

Rationally, she knew her perfectionism wasn't healthy. Her parents had never treated her like a mistake, and besides, they were dead. And she couldn't take responsibility for the fact that Trent had been a whiny, entitled kid who'd grown into a bitter, hateful man. She didn't have to do everything just right in a doomed effort to keep the peace in the family.

Yes, rationally, she knew all of that. But her objective knowledge didn't do anything to put her at ease as Tom drove like the devil himself was gaining on them.

Finally, Caroline couldn't take it anymore. She had expected a fifteen-minute car trip to a different side of town. Not this mad dash across the Great Plains. It was beginning to feel little bit like a kidnapping—one that she had been complicit in. "Where, exactly, do you live?"

"Not too much farther," he said, answering the wrong question.

But he'd actually responded, and she couldn't pass up this chance to get more out of him. "If you're spiriting me away to the middle of nowhere just to do me in, it's not going to go well for you." She didn't harbor any illusions that she could make an impact on him. He was armed and dangerous, and for all she knew, he was a black belt or something. She was good at jogging. She had taken a few self-defense classes. She wasn't going to think about how long ago, though.

That got a laugh out of him, which only made her madder. "I have no intention of killing you. Or harming you," he added as an afterthought.

"You'll forgive me if I don't find that terribly reassuring."

"Then why did you get in the car with me?"

She shook her head, not caring if he could see it or not. "I just realized that when I said something felt off at my house, you trusted me. Anyone else would've told me I was imagining things. I'm returning the favor." She leaned her head back and closed her eyes. "Don't let it go to your head."

"I doubt you'll let that happen."

The car slowed as he took an exit. But he was

going so fast that she didn't get her eyes open to see the name or number of the exit. They were literally in the middle of nowhere. She hadn't seen so much as a cow for the last—what, ten or twenty miles? It was hard to tell at the speeds they'd been traveling.

"Dare I ask how you define 'not too much farther'?"

"Are you hungry?"

She was starving, but that didn't stop her from glancing at the clock in the dashboard. The sun was low over the horizon.

"Do you always do that?" He tilted his head in her direction without making eye contact. At least, she assumed. She was beginning to hate those sunglasses. "Answer a question with an unrelated statement?"

She saw his lips twitch. "Dinner will be waiting for us. I hope pizza is all right?"

See, that was the sort of statement that made her wonder about him. He'd clearly said he was taking her to his house. Was he the kind of guy who had a personal chef? That didn't fit with the salary of an FBI agent.

But she couldn't figure out how to phrase that particular question without it sounding like an accusation. Instead, she said, "So that's a yes. And," she added before he could start laughing, "pizza is fine. Better if it has sausage and peppers on it. Mushrooms are also acceptable. Do you have any ice cream? Wine?"

"I can take care of you."

Perhaps it was supposed to be an innocent statement—a reflection of his preparedness for emergency guests. But that's not how Caroline took it.

Maybe her defenses were lower because she was tired and worried. But the moment his words filled the small space between them, her body reacted—hard. Her nipples tightened almost to the point of pain as heat flooded her stomach and pooled lower. Her toes curled, and she had to grip the handle on the passenger door to keep from moaning with raw need.

Heavens, what was with her? It had been a long day. That was all. There was no other explanation as to why a simple phrase, spoken in a particularly deep tone of voice, would have such an impact on her.

She locked the whole system down. No moaning, no shivering, and absolutely no heated glances at Tom. Besides, how would she know if his glances were heated or not? He still had on those damn sunglasses.

Instead, in a perfectly level voice, she said, "That remains to be seen, doesn't it?" She took it as a personal victory when he gripped the steering wheel with both hands.

Silence descended in the car again. If she'd had no idea where she was before, she had less now. They'd left the highway behind. The good news was that Tom was probably only doing sixty instead of breaking the sound barrier. With each turn, the roads bore less and less resemblance to an actual paved surface. But she didn't start to panic until he turned where there didn't seem to be any road at all, just a row of ragged shrubs. He opened the glove box and fished out a…remote?

"What are you doing?" she demanded.

He didn't answer. Of course he didn't. Instead, he aimed the remote at the shrubs and clicked the button.

The whole thing rolled smoothly to the side. She blinked and then blinked again. Really, her head was a mess. She was going to need a whole bottle of wine after this. "Be honest—are you Batman?"

He cracked a grin that did terrible, wonderful things to her body. Her mouth went dry and the heat that she had refused to feel before came rushing back, a hot summer wind that carried the promise of a storm. Because there was something electric in the air when he turned to face her. She wanted to lick his neck to taste the salt of his skin.

Maybe she would strip down. Her clothing was becoming unbearable. "Would you believe me if I said I was?"

She thought about that. Well, at least she tried to. Thinking was becoming hard. She was so hot. "Only if you've got an elderly British butler waiting for you."

His grin deepened and, curse her body, it responded, leaning toward him of its own volition. "I don't. Turns out elderly British butlers don't like to work off the grid in the middle of nowhere."

That got her attention. "I thought you said you had a home?" She looked around, feeling the weight of the phrase *wide-open spaces* for the first time. There was nothing around here except the highly mobile fake shrubbery. "I don't see..."

Then she saw it—in the direction where the ruts disappeared down the drive, there were trees off in the distance. "This is a real house, right? If you live in a van down by the river, I'm going to be pissed. A real house with pizza," she added. "And a real bed. I will walk back to Pierre before I crash in a sleeping bag."

It wasn't fair, that grin. His muscles weren't fair, his jaw wasn't fair and the way he had of looking at her—that, most of all, wasn't fair. Especially right now, when it was pretty obvious to everyone—all two of them—that her filters were failing her.

"I do have a housekeeper of sorts," he added, glancing at the clock in the dash. "She should have dinner underway. And in the meantime, if you'd like to swim…"

He had her at a complete disadvantage, and the hell of it was, she wasn't sure it was a bad thing. There was a part of her that desperately wanted to believe it was a good thing. At least, the part about being here with him was a good thing. There was no way to put a positive spin on someone breaking into her house and planting bugs.

"You have a pool out here?" She stared at the trees again.

"Not exactly," he said, sounding almost regretful about it. "But I have a pond—spring fed, nice and cool. If you need to cool off."

Somehow, she'd gotten close enough to him that he could cup her cheek with the palm of his hand. Her eyelashes fluttered and she couldn't help leaning into his touch. Even though this had been one of the stranger afternoons in her life, she still felt safe with him. Maybe she shouldn't. They were a million miles from nowhere. But she did.

"Let me take you home."

A pond? She didn't love mud squishing between her toes, but at this point she wasn't sure she cared. "Promise me we'll get there soon. I don't know how much longer I can wait."

She meant for the food and wine. For the cool pond. But she felt his body tense and realized that she hadn't been talking about dinner at all.

She didn't know how much longer she could wait for this man. This confusing, confounding man who cared what happened to her.

"Ten minutes. You won't regret this."

"I better not."

Neither of them moved for a second. Then, so slowly that she could feel the electricity between them crackle, he stroked his thumbs over her cheekbones. His hands were rough, but his touch was gentle and she was too tired to fight the shiver of attraction anymore.

Damn his sunglasses. Damn her exhaustion. Damn the fact that they were parked in the middle of nowhere instead of at some romantic restaurant or, even better, a bedroom. Any bedroom. Damn this corruption case she was unwillingly a part of because, better than a glass of wine and a pint of ice cream, falling into Tom Yellow Bird's arms would definitely relieve some of her stress.

He held her there, stroking her cheeks, and she thought he was going to kiss her. She wanted him to.

She also didn't—what she really wanted was for the world to go back to making sense—but that wasn't going to happen. So she'd settle for a kiss.

"We need to get going," he said, pulling away from her with what she chose to believe was reluctance. Because that way, it didn't sting as much.

"Of course," she said, staring at the trees in the distance. "Let's just go."

It almost didn't even matter where anymore.

Five

In his life, Tom had made mistakes. Beyond being unable to rescue Maggie and overlooking the fact that he should have been behind the wheel instead of Stephanie in the car accident—he had screwed up.

He'd lost the notoriously violent pimp Leonard Low Dog not once but twice and, as a result, the man had nearly killed Maggie. He'd lost the trail on Tanner Donnelly's killer until Tanner's sister, Rosebud, and her now-husband, Dan Armstrong, had cracked the case open. And Tom hadn't yet been able to uncover who was paying off judges in South Dakota.

All of those were epic errors in judgment, ones that he'd tried hard to rectify. Leonard Low Dog was serving twenty without parole. Shane Thrasher was doing forty for killing Tanner. Tom had put three judges in prison and had a hand in forcing others to retire from the bench.

But none of those mistakes were in the same category as bringing Caroline Jennings home with him.

She gasped when he finally rounded the last bend and his cabin came into view.

Aside from the Armstrongs and the Carlsons, Lilly and Joe White Thunder—people he trusted beyond the pale—he'd never brought anyone else back here. This was his sanctuary. This was where he could be close to the memories of Stephanie.

"Good God," Caroline exhaled. "Where the hell did this come from?"

"I built it." It was the summer home he and Stephanie had planned, once their careers had been established. Once they would've been able to take a month off in the summer.

And now Caroline was here. It was a mistake, but if there was one thing life had taught him, it was that there was no going back. Own up to what you did and keep moving forward. She was here, and he was sworn to protect her.

"You built it? Like, by yourself?"

"I had a few contractors, but only ones I could trust." He didn't see Lilly's pickup truck anywhere—good.

The low-slung building practically glowed in the fading sunset, the solar panels on the roofs of the house and garage glinting in the light. The panels had been a compromise. Someone could easily see his house from the air, but he was off the grid.

He hadn't exactly sworn to protect Caroline. He'd promised to take care of her. And when he'd made that promise, he'd felt the shiver pass through her body.

This was fine. Yes, he had to be in DC Monday evening, but she wouldn't be with him that long. He'd keep an eye on her this weekend until he could sweep her house. Early Monday morning, Tom would take her to work, and she'd go home Monday evening as if nothing had happened.

"This is amazing." Her voice was breathy—and that was before she turned those beautiful eyes toward him. "You live here full-time? In the middle of nowhere?"

He shrugged. "I needed a place to think. I have an apartment in Pierre, but it's not as secure."

Right. That was why he'd brought her here. Security. He would do anything to keep her safe. Even break the rules—his own rules.

Bringing her to his house? That broke every rule he'd ever set for himself. That was him putting his selfish wants ahead of his job, and that was a risk not just for him, not just for her, but for all the years he and Carlson had spent on this case. That was an unacceptable level of risk.

But what was he supposed to do? He couldn't leave her. The pull he felt to take care of her wouldn't let him. But it was more than that.

Caroline hadn't cut him a single bit of slack. Except when he'd touched her, her soft skin warm in his hands.

He pulled into the garage. It wasn't until she

gasped again that he looked at her. "Who the hell are you?" she asked, staring at his vehicles.

There were a couple of nondescript cars that he used for surveillance, his motorcycle, the old pickup truck he used when he went to the reservation and the new one he used when he was hauling supplies—not to mention his fire engine–red Corvette Stingray, which he only took out when he needed to give off an aura of wealth. "I know you may not believe this, but I don't make a habit of lying."

Based on her expression, if he thought that was going to fly, he had another thing coming. "You must not be including lying by omission in the definition."

He snorted as he got out of the car, pleased that she followed. He snagged her bags out of the trunk. "This way."

He led her to the wide porch that wrapped around three of the four sides of his house. "I have a few things I need to see to, so if you'd like to take a dip in the pond, now would be a great time." That would give him a chance to contact Carlson and see about getting her house swept for bugs.

But it'd also give him a chance to get his head back in the game. Lilly White Thunder should have gotten dinner started, and hopefully she'd had enough time to put fresh sheets on the beds.

But the thought of Caroline curled up in his bed, her hair mussed and the sheet slung low around her waist—

"Come on," he said, dropping her duffel just inside the door. The scent of pizza baking in the oven filled the cabin, but the windows were open and the house smelled fresh and clean.

As much as he loved Lilly, he was glad the older woman wasn't here. He didn't want to introduce Caroline to her, didn't want to risk the chance that Caroline's presence would slip out and make the rounds on the res.

Because that kept Caroline safer. Not because he didn't want Lilly looking at him with her warm eyes and getting any funny ideas.

Unable to help himself, he took Caroline by the hand. She was too hot and tired to meet new people, anyway. The sooner she got out of those clothes and cooled down, the better she'd be.

And her being nude had nothing to do with him. Not a damn thing.

He was rock hard as he led her through the patio doors and down a small flagstone path to where he had dammed the natural spring to create a small pool.

Caroline stumbled to a stop when she saw it. "It's…red. The water's red?"

"It is. Higher iron content. It flows into the Red Creek River," he said, stepping in close to her and pointing down the riverbanks. "That's where the name comes from. Don't worry, it won't dye your skin."

The next thing Tom knew, she whacked him on the arm. "Why didn't you tell me about this?" she demanded, her voice sounding unnaturally high. "If you had just told me you had a luxury log cabin complete with stone fireplaces and leather furniture and…"

Her voice cracked. "And a little pond that isn't even a pond." She sniffed. "You lined the bottom with stones, didn't you?"

It was the most accusatory statement he'd heard—and it wasn't about a crime or a case. It was about his little pool. "If I want to feel mud squishing in between my toes, I'll swim in the river."

She slapped him on the arm again and he let her. "You could've told me. I didn't even bring a swimsuit."

"I didn't know you needed to cool down until we were in the car." He turned his gaze out to the trees, where his spring flowed into the river. He specifically did not look at her. "If you want to soak, it's about three feet deep," he added. "Not enough to do laps."

She sighed and he glanced back at her. She was staring at that water like it was a long-lost lover that she'd never thought she'd see again. And Tom knew he was crazy, because he was suddenly jealous of the pool. "If you look, I'll gut you in your sleep," she said, sounding so tired that Tom felt like a cad.

He knew he was not an easy man to get along with. Never had been—that's why Stephanie had been so good for him. She had never let him get away with anything. She'd challenged him and pushed him and held him to a higher standard. She had met him on the playing field as an equal, and Tom had loved her for it, completely and wholly.

But even Stephanie had never threatened to gut him like a fish.

Grinning, he said, "Then I best not look."

Caroline turned away from him and grabbed the hem of her shirt, slowly lifting and revealing the pale skin of her lower back. She had the shirt halfway off and she looked at him over her shoulder and if he hadn't been lost before then, he sure as hell was now. "Shouldn't you be hiding the knives?"

"You know I'm used to sleeping with one eye open, right?" She started to lower the shirt, so he quickly took a step back. "I'm going. I won't look. I'll let you know when dinner's ready."

"At the rate we're going, it's going to be breakfast," she said with a sigh.

He turned on his heel before he did something stupid, like give in to the urge to pull her into his arms. He'd been battling that urge since he'd pulled up in front of her house that afternoon, stomach churning with dread. She'd sounded so scared on the phone—she'd been trying to laugh it off, but Tom had heard the truth in her voice. All he'd wanted to do was hold her then and make sure she knew she was safe with him.

Instead, he'd gone into her house, ready to shoot any intruder who'd stolen her peace of mind. He'd told her to pack for a weekend away and driven her way out here. She was well within her right to gut him.

And now he had to make it through the next forty-eight hours alone with her. The only things to do out here were hike and hunt, soak in the pool, and sleep. There was no television, no internet, and the only cell service was his satellite phone.

She was safe now, and he was pretty sure she knew

it. After all, wasn't she actively stripping out of her clothes? Wasn't she, at this very moment, stepping into the shallow pool he'd built, seemingly just for her? Wasn't she lowering her nude body into the water, feeling it lap at her inner thighs, her stomach, her breasts?

Jesus, how was he going to make it until Monday morning?

The water was deliciously, blissfully cold. It shocked Caroline awake and kept right on shocking her. Which was good. It was so much easier to sit and think about goose bumps than to let her mind wander over the events of the last four hours. Had it really only been four danged hours? Sheesh, what a day.

Her stomach grumbled. She would kill for a glass of wine but, bathed in the last light of dusk and letting this not-pool wash the day's sweat and anxiety away, she was content.

However, no matter how cold the water was, it couldn't erase all the heat from her body. Safely submerged beneath the waterline, her nipples were so puckered they were painful, and the heat between her legs? This water would have to be a whole lot colder before it knocked *that* down. Even though her skin was chilled, she was warm from the inside out.

She was lying naked in a pond that Tom Yellow Bird had built. She could almost pretend he'd built it for her, but she knew that was ridiculous.

Still, it was a nice fantasy. Why hadn't that man told her about this place? She could see leaving out detailed directions. He was more than a little paranoid, but maybe in his line of work, he had to be.

She floated sideways so she could get a better look at the house. She hadn't seen any sign of a maid or a housekeeper—or a British butler, for that matter. The only sign that anyone else knew where this house was had been the scent of pizza in the oven.

The house had also been spotless, as if this supposed housekeeper came in regularly to dust and air it out. Tom had hurried her through the house pretty quickly, but she'd gotten glimpses of the rough-hewn logs, a massive fireplace done in stone with a chimney that rose up to the ceiling. It was rough and overwhelming—much like Tom himself.

The whole house was a long structure, but not tall. It probably didn't even have a second story. It rode low to the ground like it didn't want to be noticed—except for the solar panels that covered the entire roof. There were trees close enough to the building to throw some shade on the porch, but otherwise, all they did was block the view from the road, however distant that was.

The logs were great behemoths of wood, and she let her imagination play over the image of Tom cutting and fitting them together like life-size Lincoln logs. Undoubtedly, he would've worked shirtless, sweat running down his neck and over his chest. Of course he would know how to use tools. And then he would lift each log into place, his muscles straining and—

"I'm coming down." His voice rang out over the plains, breaking up her reverie. "Are you decent?"

"I'm still in the water," she called back. "I… I don't have a towel or anything." And she had stripped a good six feet away from the pool because she had been so anxious to get out of her clothes. And her shoes—they weren't waterproof flip-flops. She couldn't just shove her feet back in them without ruining the leather ballerina flats, and she wasn't sure she could make it up the flagstone walk without slipping. "I may be trapped in here forever."

His laughter, deep and rich, was another pleasant surprise. She hadn't heard him laugh like that yet. "I would be a terrible host if I left you in there to turn into one giant prune. I brought you a towel."

"I haven't yet decided if you're terrible host or not. It better be a fluffy towel."

"The fluffiest. I'm not looking."

"You better not be," she said, standing slowly to let the water sheet off her body. But when she turned for the towel, she saw that he was standing by the pool, holding out the unfolded towel, his head ducked and his eyes closed. "What are you doing?" she demanded, sinking back into the water.

"The rocks are slick. I'm making sure you don't slip." He said it as if this were just an everyday occurrence instead of a giant leap of faith on her behalf.

Oh, hell—what was she talking about? How was the risk of him catching a glimpse of her nude somehow a bigger leap of faith than getting into a car with him and letting him whisk her away to the middle of nowhere?

She had already leaped. Now she just had to trust that he would catch her before she fell.

So she stood again, her skin tingling as the water rushed off it.

Moving carefully so she didn't do something embarrassing like face-plant, she stepped into the towel. His arms came around her, but he didn't step back. And he didn't open his eyes. She was so glad those damn sunglasses were gone. "You never lie?"

He shook his head. "I didn't look."

She shifted so that the towel was secured under her arms. It was a *very* fluffy towel. Then she took a deep breath and rested her hand against his cheek. His eyelashes fluttered, but they stayed closed. "Why did you bring me out here? And I don't want to hear that line about how you were keeping me safe."

"That line is the truth."

"There were a hundred ways to keep me safe inside city limits, Tom. Stop lying by omission. Why did you bring me out here?"

His hands settled around her waist, holding the towel to her body. She shivered, but it had nothing to do with the temperature of the water or the air. "I can take you back. If you want, we can leave after we eat."

She wanted to throttle him and kiss him and slap him and drop the towel. She wanted to drag him into that pool of water with her and spend time exploring. She wanted to go home and she never wanted to leave. "What if I don't want to go?"

His fingers dug into her waist, pulling her close. They were chest to chest now, her sensitive nipples scraping against the towel. Against his chest. Unconsciously, her back arched, pushing her even closer to him. "What if I want to stay?" she asked him, pushing up on her tiptoes.

"You feel it, too, don't you?" His voice was so soft she had to tilt her head to catch the words. "I never thought I'd feel this again."

Again? What the hell did that mean, *again*? He'd brought her here on the pretense of protecting her!

She pulled away from him—but she didn't get far. Her feet slid out from under her and she started to fall—but the impact never came. Instead, she found herself swept into Tom's arms as if she were something precious.

"Whoa," she said, impressed despite herself. It was ridiculous because this entire situation was ridiculous. Tom Yellow Bird was literally sweeping her off her feet. "You can put me down now."

"I didn't bring you all the way out here for you to crack your head on the stone pavers," he said, his voice the very picture of cool, calm and collected. And he did not put her down.

She had no choice but to lock her arms around his neck. "Why did you bring me out here?"

It took a lot to rattle Tom. He'd stared down cold-blooded killers and talked his way out of more than a few bad situations.

But catching a damp Caroline in his arms? Cradling her to his chest? Carrying her all the way inside and then setting her down and turning his back instead of heading straight into the bedroom and spending the rest of the night feasting on her body instead of dinner?

His hands shook—*shook*, damn it—as he stoked the fire in the pit. Then, when he judged that she'd had enough time to get dressed, he opened the wine and carried it down to where he'd arranged the patio chairs around the little table close enough to the fire that the worst of the bugs would stay away. It was better to focus on these tiny details than what was happening inside his bedroom.

Or what he wanted to happen in his bedroom.

Finally, he couldn't take it anymore. He took a healthy pull of his wine. Normally he didn't drink much. He didn't like having his senses dulled.

Right now? Yeah, he needed to be significantly less aware. Less aware of Caroline's scent combined with the fresh smell of the spring. Or of her weight in his arms or the bare skin at the back of her knees where he'd held her. He wanted to lick her there and see if she was ticklish—but he didn't dare.

Damn it all. He was failing at thinking about Caroline with any sense of rationality. So he did the only thing he could—he thought of the one person who could always hold his attention, who got him through the worst of the stakeouts and helped him sleep after the bad days.

Stephanie. His wife.

God, she had been too perfect for this world. The

first time he'd seen her in that formfitting white dress, her jet-black hair and vivid blue eyes turning every head in the room…

Oh, he could still see the way her whole face lit up when they made eye contract. He could still feel that spark that had lit in his chest as he'd cut through the crowd to get to her—the spark that had told him she was *it*. That woman, whoever she was, was his forever and ever, until death did them part.

But for the first time in a long time—years, even—that memory of Stephanie didn't hold his attention. Instead of lingering in the past, he couldn't escape the present.

He heard the patio door swish open, then closed. He heard the sound of tentative footsteps crossing the porch and moving down the two stairs. He heard the evening breeze sigh through the grasses and the gentle burbling of his spring as it flowed out of his pool and made its way down to the river.

And when Caroline took her seat, he turned, and damn it, there was that spark again, threatening to jump the barriers he'd tried to erect around it, threatening to catch in the prairie grass, burning everything in its path. Including him.

Caroline wasn't Stephanie. Stephanie wouldn't have been caught dead in a pair of old cutoff shorts and a faded gray T-shirt. Flip-flops would have never crossed Stephanie's toes. Stephanie wouldn't have been seen with her hair curling damply around her shoulders. And Stephanie never would have picked up the empty glass and said, "There better be some of that left for me."

"I told you," he replied, filling her glass, "I'm not a terrible host. I'll be right back with the pizza."

He plated up the pizza and snagged some napkins. God bless Lilly for pulling something together on such short notice.

Caroline hadn't moved from her spot, except to draw up her feet. She wasn't perfect. But by God, the woman looked like she fit out here. "Sausage," he said, handing over her plate.

She took the pizza, and for a while, neither of them spoke. Tom was used to ignoring hunger when he was on a stakeout and delivery would have blown his cover, but Lilly had, once again, made just what he wanted, almost by magic.

He knew it was coming, though. Caroline was not going to sit quietly over there for long. Finally, she set her plate aside and turned to face him. "So?"

"So?" he agreed, refilling both their glasses. "You have questions?"

"You're damn right I do." It could have come out snappish—but it didn't. Her voice took on a languid tone, one that matched the hazy quality of the fire. "Explain this house to me."

"Like I said—I built it."

"By yourself."

"That's correct." He waited, but he knew he wouldn't have to wait long.

He didn't. She was sharp, his Caroline. "With what money? Because that was one of the nicest bathrooms

I've ever been in—and it's not like Minneapolis has a lack of decent bathrooms. And the kitchen—it's a chef's wet dream."

He laughed and she laughed with him, but he knew he wasn't off the hook. "Quality is often worth the price."

There was something sharp about her eyes, and he wished he could see her in action in the courtroom as a lawyer. Not from behind the bench, but in front of it. "But that's just it. Who's paying for it? An FBI agent doesn't make this kind of money—no matter how special you are. You have a top-of-the-line cabin on what I can only assume is a pretty big spread of land."

"Eighty acres from the road to the edge of the Red Creek Reservation. I grew up about thirty miles from here." He met her gaze. "I enjoy my privacy."

He could see her thinking over that information. "You maintain an apartment in Pierre."

"And one in Rapid City." Her eyes got wide. "I have a lot of territory to cover. Plus, I have a safe house in Pierre where I can hide people for a while." Only after he said it did he realize what he'd just admitted.

He could have put her in the safe house. Sure, it might have been uncomfortable for a judge to suddenly find herself bunking with former prostitutes and recovering drug addicts, but she would have been perfectly secure.

Instead, he'd brought her out here.

"In the interest of full disclosure," he added with a wave of his hand.

"About damn time," she murmured. But again, she didn't sound angry about it. She was looking at him with those beautiful eyes and suddenly he couldn't figure out why he hadn't told her all this up front. "You own all these various and sundry properties?"

"Yup." He stretched his legs out toward the fire and, amazingly, felt some of the tension of the afternoon begin to drift away, like embers in the wind.

He was not a man who relaxed. There were too many criminals to track and arrest. He'd made so many enemies just doing his job that he rarely let his guard down.

But here? Sitting by a fire with a pretty woman on a clear summer night, a bottle of wine to share?

"Who paid for it?" she asked, her voice curious without being accusatory.

"My wife."

Six

She hadn't just heard that, had she?

"Your *wife*?" Well, that certainly made sense with the "again" comment from earlier. He was married. Of course he was. So what had happened down by the pool? "Where is she?"

He dropped his gaze to his wineglass. "Buried next to her grandparents in Washington, DC."

The air whooshed out of Caroline's lungs. "I'm sorry." Could she be any bigger of an idiot? She might as well have accused him of adultery.

He shrugged, but his face was carefully blank—just like it'd been on the stand when that defense lawyer had tried to trick him. "She died nine years ago in a car accident—hit by a drunk driver. I should have been behind the wheel—but I'd stayed at the party. I had some business to deal with."

The way he said *business* sent a shiver down Caroline's back. She had the distinctive feeling that he hadn't been getting stock tips.

"In DC?"

He nodded and leaned back, his eyes on the stars. Caroline followed his gaze, and what she saw took her breath away. The night sky was unbelievably gorgeous, not a single star dimmed by city lights.

"The FBI was my way off the res," he began. "But I wasn't alone. Rosebud, the little sister of my best friend, Tanner, got a scholarship to Georgetown and we stuck together—two Lakota fish way out of water."

Caroline had some questions but decided that, since Tom was actually talking, she'd best not interrupt him.

"She and Carlson were in class together and started dating—she's the lawyer for the Red Creek tribe now. James and I got along, and he made sure I went with them to all the fancy parties that his parents made him attend. It always struck me as an odd way to rebel, but..." He shrugged. "That's how I met Stephanie."

He spoke with such tenderness that, once again, Caroline felt like an idiot. He'd loved his wife. Was it wrong to be jealous of a dead woman? Because she couldn't help but be envious of the woman who could hold Tom Yellow Bird's heart.

"She and Carlson were childhood friends—I think their mothers wanted them to marry, but they both settled on two dirt-poor Indians with no money and no family names." He laughed, as if that were funny. "Carlson came west because Rosebud and I needed his help with this case, and he met Maggie—it's quite a story. Ask Maggie about it sometime." A melancholy silence settled over him. "He treats her well, which is good."

The way he said it made it clear that if Tom didn't think Carlson was treating his wife well, there'd be bloodshed. "So you've been working with Carlson for…how long?"

Belatedly, she realized what else he'd said. He'd just assumed that she would meet one of his oldest friends. Maggie probably knew all his embarrassing childhood stories, every dumb and brilliant thing he'd ever done. Carlson was Tom's most trusted friend.

And Tom had just made the assumption that Caroline would meet them. More than that, that she'd meet his friends in a social setting instead of in a law office or a courtroom.

Almost as if Tom expected to be doing a lot more of this—sitting out under the stars, having wine and pizza, and talking—with Caroline.

"We've known each other for over fourteen years now."

Nine years since Stephanie died—Caroline did the quick math.

Tom looked at her. "I was married for almost four years. Since I know you're trying to figure it out."

"That's not the only thing I'm trying to figure out," she murmured. "She was well-off?"

"Her mother was an heiress and her father was a senator." He exhaled heavily. "We tried not to talk politics. They did their best to accept me, which is more than a lot of people in their place might have done. But I was from a different world." He was quiet for a moment, and Caroline couldn't figure out if he was done or if he was just thinking. "I still am."

"I'll give you that—this place is different." She looked back at the stars, galaxies spread out before her, their depths undimmed by something as innocuous as fluorescent lighting.

A little like the man next to her. She topped off her glass and his when he held it out. "I'm sorry about your wife," she said again, because it seemed like the thing to say—even though it wasn't enough. He'd lost someone he cared for, and that was painful no matter what. She reached over and gave his hand a squeeze. He squeezed back, lacing his fingers with hers.

Neither of them pulled away.

"So this was all because of her money?"

"I invested wisely. She ran a charity. Her mother still runs it." He opened his mouth, as if he were going to expand upon that statement, but then he shook his head and changed the subject. "How about you?" He lolled his head to the side, and for a moment, he looked younger. The faint lines of strain were gone from around his eyes and his mouth was relaxed. He looked ten years younger. "Any dead husbands—or other bodies—in your closet?"

She kept her face even. As much as she didn't want to turn the spotlight back onto her occasionally questionable choices, she was relieved that they weren't going to keep talking about his late wife. "Nope. I always figured that once my career was established, I'd settle down, start a family. I've got time."

A look of pure sadness swept over his features before he went back to staring at the sky. "I used to think the same thing."

She didn't like that sadness. "I was almost engaged once, in college," she heard herself say, which surprised her. She never told anyone about Robby. "We were young and stupid and thought we could make it work, us against the world. But we couldn't even make it through senior year." That was glossing over things quite a bit.

The truth of the matter was that she and Robby couldn't make it past a pregnancy scare. She hated making mistakes, and that particular one had nearly altered the entire course of her life.

She and Robby had talked about getting married in that wishful-thinking way all kids did when they were crazy in lust, but when her period had been three days late…

She shuddered at the memory and once again gave thanks that it had been stress, not pregnancy, that had thrown her cycle off.

"Things didn't go as planned," she admitted, which was a nice way of saying that when she'd told Robby she was late, he'd all but turned tail and bolted for the door. The fantasy of living happily ever after with him had crumbled before her eyes, and she'd known then that she'd made the biggest mistake of her life—up to that point, anyway.

Which was ironic, considering that Trent's nickname for her when she'd been growing up had been "the mistake." Not that her parents had ever treated her like that, but Trent had. He would have loved it if Caroline had made the exact same mistake in her own life. "I thought it was going to be perfect, but all it turned out to be was heartbreak."

"You didn't marry him, though?"

"Nope."

Tom shrugged. "No one's perfect—especially not in relationships."

Oh, if only it were that simple. "Regardless, I don't tell people about that. It reflects poorly on my judgment, you understand."

"Of course. I imagine he couldn't keep up with you."

She chuckled at that. "If I agree with you, it'll make me sound egotistical."

His laughter was warm and deep, and it made her want to curl into him. "Perish the thought."

Long moments passed. She sipped her wine, feeling the stress of the day float away on a pleasant buzz. He didn't think less of her because she'd almost tied herself to the wrong man.

Maybe he wouldn't think less of her because she'd made a mistake trusting the wrong man.

"Tom?"

"Yeah?"

"You still haven't answered my question."

Why was she here? What was going on between them? Because she couldn't imagine that he brought other potential witnesses out here and let them skinny-dip in the pond and hold his hand under the stars.

She wanted to think this was different, that he was different with her. Not like he was with his socialite wife in the rarefied air of DC politics and power—but not like he was when he was stalking bad guys and saving the world.

It wasn't egotistical—it was *selfish* to want a little bit of Tom Yellow Bird all to herself. But she did. In this time, this place—hidden away from the rest of the world—she wanted him. Not as a protector and not as a law-enforcement colleague—but as something else. Something *more*.

It was worse than selfish. It was stupid, a risk she shouldn't even contemplate taking.

So why was she contemplating it so damn hard? God, it'd been such a long time since she'd risked letting off a little steam with some good sex. And out here, so far removed from neighbors and courtrooms…

It felt like they'd left reality behind and she and Tom were in a bubble, insulated from the real world and any real consequences.

Would it be so bad to let herself relax for a little bit? Tom would be amazing, she knew. And now that she'd seen where he lived—how he lived—she trusted that no one would ever know what happened between them. No nefarious stalkers planting bugs here. Tom simply wouldn't allow it.

Surely, she thought, staring at his profile, she could enjoy a little consensual pleasure with him without ruining everything, couldn't she? Take the necessary precautions, not let her heart get involved—not compromise the case?

He didn't answer for a long time. Then, suddenly he stood. "It's late," he said, his voice gruff as he pulled her to her feet. "Let me show you your room."

Yes, she wanted more—but it was clear that, at least right now, she wasn't going to get it.

Tom had always liked this bed. This was a top-of-the-line memory-foam mattress—king size, with fifteen-hundred-thread-count sheets. The ceiling fan spun lazily overhead, making the temperature bearable. Dinner had been delicious and the wine excellent. This was as close to peace and quiet as he got.

So why couldn't he sleep?

Because. Caroline was at the other end of the hall.

He forced himself to be still and let his mind drift. Even if he couldn't sleep, he could rest, and that was all he needed. He didn't need to be on full alert. He had a lazy weekend ahead of him. He just needed enough to keep himself—and his dick—under control.

He let his mind go over his plans for Monday. A morning flight to Washington—it was the only flight, so he hadn't had much of a choice there. Then he'd have dinner with Senator and Mrs. Rutherford—his in-laws. From there, they'd go to the gala fund-raiser for the Rutherford Foundation, the charity Stephanie had founded with her trust fund money. Celine Rutherford, Stephanie's mother, ran the foundation in her daughter's name, but Tom liked to help out whenever he could. It was his way of honoring his late wife.

He didn't love gala fund-raisers, because he'd never quite gotten over the feeling that he was an interloper. He didn't love going back to DC for the same reason, although if he went for work, he was usually fine. And while he greatly respected the Rutherfords, seeing them was still painful. Celine strongly resembled her daughter, and it hurt Tom to look at her and know that was what Stephanie would have looked like if they'd gotten the chance to grow old together.

Usually, he didn't go back for these sorts of things. He had cases to solve, bad guys to catch—and the Rutherfords understood that. They never questioned Tom's work ethic. Instead, they all seemed content with chatty emails from Celine every month or so, plus cards at the holidays.

But once a year, he made the trip out East. He sat down with the Rutherfords and celebrated his wife's life and legacy. The Rutherford Foundation was dedicated to furthering education for girls and women around the world, and thanks to Tom's involvement, he'd gotten some of those funds allocated to Native American reservations around the US.

The timing *sucked.* When he'd made the executive decision to bring Caroline out here, he'd reasoned that he'd have plenty of time to get her back, get the equipment he needed and sweep her house. But in talking with Carlson while she'd soaked in his pool, Tom had realized he wouldn't be able to make his flight if he swept the house himself. As it was, they were going to have to get up before the crack of dawn on Monday so he'd have enough time to get back to his place in Pierre and grab his tuxedo.

At least Carlson could do the sweep on Monday. Tom would feel better if he checked every inch of Caroline's house himself, but he trusted Carlson implicitly. After this, Tom was getting his own sweeper. To hell with using the department's. The things he could buy on the internet were almost as good. Good enough to have checked Caroline's house, anyway.

All these plans buzzed through his head as he lay there, which was fine. It was much better to think of airport security lines and tuxedos than it was to dwell on the mental image of Caroline lying nude in his pool.

He'd left her out there for almost twenty minutes while he'd called Carlson and gotten the pizzas Lilly had made out of the oven. And the whole time, he hadn't been thinking about his late wife or about gala fund-raisers. In all actuality, he'd barely been thinking about corrupt judges or bugged houses.

All he'd been able to think about was Caroline. Lying nude in his pool.

Even now, he could see her out there, the hazy golden light of sunset glimmering around her hair, the reddish spring water dancing over her skin. God, she must have been gorgeous. But he hadn't looked. He'd promised.

At some point in the still of the night, he became aware of movement. Wild animals sometimes prowled around at night—the smell of pizza could've drawn them. Without moving, he woke up and listened.

The sound he heard—the regular if light sound of footsteps, the faint squeaking of the floorboards, the sound of a knob turning—weren't coming from outside. He didn't react as Caroline stepped into the room. Instead, all he could think was that he hoped she didn't gut him like a fish.

He waited until, nearly noiselessly, she'd made her way over to him. "I told you I was a light sleeper."

She made a little noise of surprise. "You're awake?"

"So are you."

"I…" He heard her take a deep breath. "I couldn't sleep."

That got his eyes open. "Yeah?"

But the sight of her in a short cotton gown that fell to just above her knees, her hair rumpled with sleep—God, he didn't know if he could be this strong. "Do you really think someone is going to try and blackmail me?"

"No guarantees in life, but probably. Do you have something to hide?" He desperately wanted her to say no. Maybe it was because it was late or maybe it was because he hadn't been able to stop thinking about her since he'd seen her in her courtroom, ferocious and beautiful.

Or maybe it was just because she was standing in

his bedroom in the dead of night, looking for reassurance. And if there was one thing Tom could provide, it was reassurance. Hands-on, physical reassurances. A lot of them.

For years—*years*—he had put all his energy into doing the job, because what else did he have? Not his wife. Not the family they'd planned for.

All he had was the never-ending quest for truth, justice and the American way. He gave the FBI nearly everything he had, and what he held back, he gave to rescuing girls from prostitution.

No matter what, he wanted Caroline to be honest and true. And he wanted her all for himself, selfish bastard that he was. He wanted Caroline for himself, not because she was a new lead or a key component of this damnable case.

He wanted her. God, it felt so good to want again. Even better to be wanted.

There was a pause that made him wonder if maybe he'd read the situation wrong. Then she said, "I don't have any kinks." He heard her swallow. "At least, I don't think I do..."

Tom's body was instantly awake. "You're not sure?"

"Who can say if it's something that's going to be used against me?"

Moving slowly, he sat up, ignoring the way his body jumped to attention. "I could," he offered, not even bothering to convince himself that it was knowledge necessary to keep her safe. This had nothing to do with protecting her, and they both knew it. "You could tell me what you like and I'll let you know if it's a hazard to your reputation or not."

He heard her swallow again, the soft click of her throat muscles working. Would she turn and go back to her bedroom, shut the door and lock it? Or would she…

"I like men," she began, her voice so soft he almost couldn't hear the waver in it.

So far, so good. "Just men?"

He could see her head bob—thank God for the full moon tonight.

"Nothing illegal about that. I think it makes you normal. Unless…" He breathed deeply. He would not lose control. Simple as that. "Do you do anything with your partner that might be dangerous?"

He saw her chest rise and fall as she exhaled. "I… I like to be on top. I have been told that I have extremely sensitive breasts. I like it when my lover strokes them and sucks them. But not biting—they're too sensitive for that."

Adrenaline slammed through his system, his heart pounding and his dick throbbing. He could see it in his mind's eye, her riding him, his face buried in her breasts. "That doesn't seem unusual." His voice cracked.

He needed to have her over him. He needed to feel the warm wetness of her body surrounding him, holding him. He needed to pull one of her nipples into his mouth and suck on it until she screamed with pleasure.

God, he wasn't sure he had ever needed anything so much in his entire life.

He didn't dare move. He didn't want to break the spell that had her sharing her deepest desires. "Is there anything else that could be considered unusual?"

"I..." She took a step toward him. It wasn't a big movement, but he felt it down to his toes. That spark that had always existed between them—it was no longer an isolated flash of light in the darkness. It was burning hotter and brighter than anything he'd ever felt before. It lit him up. *She* lit him up. "I like it when a man bends me over and takes me from behind."

For all of his years keeping his emotions blank and unreadable, Tom could not fight back the groan that started low in his chest and burned its way out of his throat. "Yeah?" he choked out.

"That's not dangerous, is it?" Her voice shook again, but it didn't sound like nerves. It sounded like *want*. "I sometimes fantasize about a man coming into my chambers and bending me over my desk because he wants me so much that we can't wait. He—he might hold me by my hair or dig his fingers into my skin. He can't even wait to get undressed." She took a shuddering breath. "Is it wrong, do you think? It's so risky..."

"Wrong?" He laughed, a dry sound. "I've never heard anything so right in my entire life." Her face practically glowed with what looked a hell of a lot like relief. "I wouldn't try it until your office has been swept for bugs, though. And only with a man you trust completely."

She took another small step closer. His breath caught in his throat—he could see her legs now, long and bare. She had an unearthly glow where the moonlight kissed her skin. He'd never been jealous of the moon before. "That's the problem, you see? There aren't very many men I trust."

"There aren't?"

She shook her head. "Only you."

Tom was on his feet before he could think better of it. Then she was in his arms and he was kissing her.

No, *kissing* was too generic a word that covered too many things.

It didn't cover this—he was *consuming* her. He devoured her lips and sucked on her tongue while he ran his hands down her back and over her bottom, squeezing hard.

"Anything else," he whispered in her ear before he sucked her lobe in between his teeth and nipped, "that could be used against you?"

"I don't like prissy, cautious sex." Her body was vibrating in his arms, and he could feel her nipples, pointed and scraping against his chest. "I like it wild and rough. Loud and—"

He couldn't take another moment of this exquisite torture. He swept her legs out from under her for the second time in a few short hours and threw her onto the bed. "I wanted to do this earlier," he told her. "But I didn't know what you wanted."

"You." He grabbed at his T-shirt. Her hands went

to the waistband of his shorts, shoving them and his briefs down. It wasn't gentle or patient. He grabbed the hem of her nightshirt and yanked it over her head, leaving her bare before him just as his erection sprang free. She gasped and then palmed him. Desire ran ragged through him.

When she looked up at him, her eyes luminous in the moonlight, she said, "I want you. Because I feel it, too."

Tom paused for just a second, a wild look of need in his eyes, and Caroline wondered if she'd said the wrong thing.

Please, she found herself praying as she clung to him, *please don't let this be a mistake.*

It wouldn't be, and that was final. She wasn't a naive college girl living in her own little world anymore. She and Tom were consenting adults and it was perfectly reasonable to burn off a little excess energy doing consensual things. What happened in this room had nothing to do with corruption or cases or the errors of her ways.

But the next thing she knew, Tom had pulled free of her grasp and fallen to his knees. Her hands were empty and she felt oddly bereft.

He grabbed her by the hips and hauled her to the edge of the bed, his fingers digging into her skin. "Caroline," he groaned and then his teeth skimmed over her inner thigh. "Did you ever think of this?"

Then his mouth was upon her, licking and sucking her tender flesh. She sank her fingers into his hair and gave herself up to the sensation. Tom shifted, lifting her legs over his shoulders and spreading her wider for his attentions.

"Sometimes," she got out in a breathy voice. But not very often.

Oral sex was just…one of those things. Her previous lovers had either not been enthusiastic about it or hadn't been good—the worst was when it was both combined. They would go down on her for a few minutes and consider that an even exchange for fellatio.

But Tom? Not only was he enthusiastic—and that would've been more than enough—but he knew what he was doing. He found the bud of her sex and tormented it relentlessly with his tongue. One hand snaked up over her stomach until he was fondling her breast, rubbing his callused thumb over her nipple until it ached. His other hand? When he slipped a finger inside her, she almost came off the bed. She wanted to cry with satisfaction. She didn't. Instead, she just held on for the ride.

Jesus, her fantasies weren't this good. Tom found a rhythm and worked her body. He teased her nipple and licked her sex and thrust his fingers into her body. He gave her no quarter, no space for her mind to wander off and debate the wisdom of this. He kept her in the here and now, in this bedroom, with him. He pushed her body relentlessly as the orgasm built. He must've been able to tell she was close, because suddenly, he wasn't just flicking his thumb back and forth over her taut nipple—he pinched it between his thumb and finger and made a humming noise deep in the back of his throat.

Caroline came undone. Her thighs clenched around his fingers as she rode the waves of pleasure until they left her sated and limp. Slowly, Tom withdrew. He went from licking to pressing gentle kisses against her sex. Instead of pinching her nipple, he stroked his fingers all around her breast and then down over her stomach. Slowly, he pulled free of her body. She shivered at the loss.

She felt she needed to say something, show her appreciation somehow. She should be polite and reciprocate, at least.

But she found she couldn't do any of those things. She was boneless with satisfaction, able to do little more than smile at him. "Hopefully," she said, her voice sultry even to her own ears, "that wasn't a hazardous activity."

Tom got to his feet. The moonlight kissed his skin, giving him an otherworldly look. His erection jutted out from his body, and she lifted her foot to nudge at the tip. "No," he said, his voice deep and commanding, "I don't think there was anything damaging about that." He grabbed her foot when she nudged him again and lifted it, pressing a kiss to the sole.

It tickled and she laughed.

He leaned over her, holding his body above hers. The scent of sex hung between them as his erection brushed her hip. Unexpectedly, her eyes watered. This man—more than his dammed spring, more than his wine and pizza—she'd needed this from this man. "You decide."

She touched his face, letting her fingertips trace the map of his skin. "On what?"

Even in this dim light, she could see his eyes darken. "Do I flip you over or make you ride me?" She gasped at his words, her body arching into his. He'd paid attention, bless the man. He went on, "Should I suck your breasts or slap your ass?"

She pulled him down onto the bed, rolling as he went. "I'm on top."

"God," he muttered, shifting so they were in the middle of the bed, "I love a woman who knows what she wants."

Seven

"Condoms? Something?"

It took a second for Caroline's words to sink in, because Tom was having trouble getting past the way she straddled him, her breasts ripe for the plucking. His erection ached with need—and it only got worse when she settled her weight on him. He could feel the warmth of her sex against his dick—so close, yet so far away. He flexed his hips, dragging against her sensitive skin.

She made a noise high in the back of her throat as she shifted, bringing him against her entrance. But before he could thrust home, she leaned up, breaking the contact. "*Tom.* Condom?"

"Um..." Right, right. Birth control was the responsible thing here. As much as he hated to lift Caroline off him, he couldn't risk her health just because he couldn't think of a single thing beyond how her body would take his in. "One second."

He kept a fully stocked emergency cabinet in the storeroom that could help him survive a few months out here—and along with the necessities in the kit were unlubricated condoms. He just had to find them—which he had to do naked, while not looking at the pictures on the wall.

As he searched, Tom could almost feel Stephanie's eyes on him. Which was ridiculous. But he couldn't bring himself to glance at their wedding photos. He couldn't display them out in the open, but he also couldn't put them in an album on the shelf. So they lived here, in his storage room.

She would've wanted him to do this, he told himself, rifling through the emergency supplies. Stephanie had loved him beyond the point of reason, and she wouldn't have wanted him to spend the rest of his life alone. Not that having sex with Caroline had anything to do with the rest of his life. Those two things weren't directly connected.

Except…for that spark.

Stephanie would have wanted him to be happy. Polished, quiet Stephanie, who liked slow seductions and quiet submissions and sex in a bed. Only a bed. Never in an office or on a desk.

Finally, he found the condoms and a tube of all-purpose lube. It felt like he'd been looking for hours, but it'd probably been no more than five minutes.

By the time he made it back to the bedroom, he was afraid the magic of the moment had been broken.

He paused at the bedroom door, trying to play out all possible outcomes. Would she have fallen back asleep? Changed her mind? Would he have to go sit in his spring-fed pool to keep himself under control?

He could take care of himself—he'd been doing it for years. But he didn't want to. He wanted to get back to that place where he and Caroline were two consenting adults about to get what they needed.

He needed her.

He had from the very beginning, when she'd been magnificent in her courtroom.

"Tom?" Her voice was soft, sultry. Not the voice of a judge, but the voice of a woman. A woman who needed to be satisfied.

For a fleeting second, he wished he were bringing a little more experience to the table. He didn't want to think he'd forgotten how to do this, but it'd been a long, long time since he'd had sex with another person.

But then he licked his lips, the taste of her sex still on his mouth, and he figured, what the hell. Sex was like riding a bike, only a lot more fun. "I'm here."

She was splayed out on her side, moonlight kissing her in the most intimate of places. Places he'd kissed. Places he was going to kiss again.

He watched as she slid a hand over her breast, cupping it and stroking her own nipple. He went painfully hard at the sight as her head lolled back. "Did you find a condom?" she asked in a breathy voice.

Instantly, he was hard all over again. His mind might have some performance anxiety, but his body was raring to go. "I found several."

"Oh, thank God." She pushed herself up and patted the bed next to her. "Come to bed, Tom."

He dropped the supplies on the sheets and crawled over to her. "You look good in my bed," he murmured, rolling onto his back. "I like you there."

He reached for the condom—but before he could, her mouth was on him. "Caroline," he groaned, trying to pull her up.

"You didn't tell me what you liked," she said, her voice throaty as she licked up his length.

He sank his fingers into her hair, trying to pull her up and trying to hold her where she was at the same time. His brain short-circuited as the unfamiliar sensations rocketed through him. Her mouth was warm and wet and she was just as fierce as he'd hoped.

"This…this is good," he ground out, his hips moving on their own. She gripped him tightly as she licked at his tip. "God, Caroline."

Then he looked down at her. She was staring up at him as she licked and sucked, a huge grin on her face as she pleasured him. "This isn't a hazardous activity, is it?"

He wasn't going to make it. He sat up and pulled her away. He needed the barrier of the condom between them, because it was too much—she was too much. "I can't wait," he told her, rolling on the condom and applying the lube. "I need you right now."

"Yes," she hissed, straddling him again. This time,

when his erection found her opening, she didn't pull away. Instead, she lowered her weight onto him, slowly at first, and then, with a moan that made his gaze snap to hers, she sank down the rest of the way, taking him in fully. "Oh, *yes*, Tom."

His mind blanked in the white-hot pleasure of it all. It'd been so long—but his body hadn't forgotten. The smell of sex hung heavy around them, and Caroline's body pinned him to the bed. He blinked, bringing her into focus. He let go of her hips only long enough to shove the pillows under his shoulders.

Because he hadn't forgotten what she'd whispered to him. "These are amazing," he told her, doing his best to focus on her needs, her body—and not how he was already straining to keep his climax in check. He stroked his fingertips over her breasts. "Simply amazing."

Her back arched as her hips began to rock. "Do you like them?"

"I do. But," he added, reaching around her waist with one hand and pushing her down to his mouth, "I like them more here."

With that, he sucked her right breast into his mouth and teased her left nipple with his fingers. He didn't bite—but he didn't have to. Caroline went wild as he lavished attention on her breasts. She moaned as her flesh filled his mouth, his hands. He wasn't gentle, either. She wanted loud? She wanted to feel like he couldn't hold back?

It wasn't a stretch, that. He lost himself in her body, her sounds, her taste. She grabbed onto the headboard and rode him wildly. It was all he could do to hang on long enough.

But he did. When she threw her head back and screamed out his name, he dug his fingers into the smooth skin of her hips and, thrusting madly, let go. God, it felt so good to let go again.

She collapsed onto his chest, panting heavily as he wrapped his arms around her and held on tight. In that moment, he felt like he'd come home again.

Who knew that by losing himself in her, he'd find himself again? But he was alive from head to toe, truly *alive*.

"Tom," she whispered against the crook of his neck.

"Yeah." He exhaled heavily and wished he were a younger man, one who had it in him to roll her onto her back and take her again. He shifted, lifting her off enough that he could get rid of the condom before settling her back against his chest. "Wow."

After a long time—Tom had begun to drift—she propped herself up on her elbows. "So," she said, the happiest smile he'd seen yet on her face. "What are the plans for the rest of the weekend?"

And then, because he wasn't as old as he thought, he did roll her onto her back and cover her with his body. "This," he said, flexing his hips and grinding against her. "Pizza and wine and the pool and *this*, Caroline."

"Finally," she murmured against his lips as she wrapped her legs around his waist. "A straight answer."

He was already thrusting inside her when he realized that the sensation was more intense than it'd been last time. He withdrew long enough to get another condom before he buried his body in hers again.

He'd finally come home, and he damn well intended to stay here.

Eight

This was a mistake, Tom thought as he stood next to the bed, staring down at Caroline's sleeping form. A rare tactical error. A series of errors, each compounding the other until what he was left with was a huge mess of his own making.

He shouldn't have brought her out here, knowing damn well he had to fly out of South Dakota first thing Monday morning. And he shouldn't have fallen into bed with her, either.

But he'd done both of those things, anyway. For once, he hadn't put the case first. And now he had to deal with the consequences.

She wasn't going to like this.

"Caroline."

She startled, blinking sleepily at him in the soft light from the bedside lamp. "What? Time to get up?"

"Yes."

Tom handed over the cup of coffee. She sat up to take it, which made the sheet fall down around her waist. He almost groaned at the sight of her breasts. Damn it, this was not how he'd wanted to wake her up, either. But the die was cast.

She smiled sleepily at him, an invitation and a promise all rolled into one. "How much time do we have?"

He gritted his teeth. He'd indulged himself all weekend long. That was a luxury neither of them had right now. "Get dressed."

She blinked at him. At least this time, her eyes were almost moving at the same speed. "Are we back to this? You're not going to answer any question directly? Come on, babe."

Crap. It wasn't even five fifteen in the morning, and all he wanted to do was climb back into this bed with her and forget about the rest of the world, just like he'd dared to do for the last two days.

The rest of the world, however, wasn't about to be forgotten. He sat down on the bed. Which was a mistake, because when he did that, he reached over and cupped her cheek. "There's been a change of plans."

She leaned into his touch, looking worried. He didn't like that look. "How bad is it?"

There was probably a diplomatic way to inform her of the change in their travel plans. But he didn't have time to figure out what it was. "You're coming to Washington, DC, with me."

Her mouth fell open, and she jolted so hard she almost spilled her coffee. "But I'm supposed to be at work today..."

Tom forced himself to stand and move away from her. "There's been an emergency. Your house will not be secure by the time you get off work today, and I'm not willing to risk you going back there without having it swept. So you're coming with me."

She blinked again and then, in one long swallow, finished the coffee. When the mug was empty, she smiled widely. "Funny. Real funny, Tom. It's a little early for practical jokes, but it's good to see that you have a sense of humor at any hour." Her voice trailed off when he didn't return her easy grin. "Wait—you aren't joking?"

He shook his head. "This trip has been planned for months. I thought I'd be able to secure your house before my flight left this morning, but when I realized I wouldn't have time, Carlson was going to do it for me. But he's had an emergency and I don't trust anyone else to do it."

The ticket desk at the Pierre Airport wasn't open yet, so he'd have to buy her ticket when he got there. He hadn't once been on a full flight from Pierre to Minneapolis to Dulles, so it shouldn't be a problem.

"I have to go to DC because you have to go to DC," she repeated, as if she were trying to learn a foreign language. He nodded. "Because the only other person you trust to sweep my house for bugs that may or may not exist is dealing with an emergency."

"That's correct."

She flung off the covers, and despite the early hour, despite the less-than-ideal circumstances, his pulse beat a little harder as she stomped around his bedroom wearing nothing.

"I have cases on the docket," she announced, her voice suddenly loud. The caffeine must have kicked in. "I can't just jet off with you. There has to be someone else—"

"No, there isn't. I told you—Carlson and I keep our activities quiet. That way no one can compromise our investigations. His wife is having pregnancy complications and I'm not about to mess with our operating procedures—procedures that have led to several successful convictions—just because—"

"You're being ridiculous," she snapped, throwing on her clothes.

Maybe he was. Maybe he shouldn't be taking her anywhere. After all, it hadn't taken more than a few hours out here, away from prying eyes and ears, before they'd wound up in bed together. It was one thing to indulge in a long, satisfying weekend with her at his isolated cabin—it was something completely different to take her to DC.

Then, before he could come up with any sort of witty retort to "ridiculous," she pulled up short. "Wait—Maggie's having complications?" She spun on him. "Is she okay?"

The fact that she was suddenly concerned for one of

his oldest friends—whom she did not know—despite the fact that she was furious with him made something tighten in his chest. "She's got the very best watching over her. She's had some problems with high blood pressure, but they're controlling it." He hoped like hell Maggie would be okay. He couldn't bear the thought of losing another woman he cared for.

"That's good. I hope she's okay. But I can't fly to Washington, Tom."

"Take a sick day. Two," he corrected. "We'll fly back tomorrow."

She jammed her hands on her hips. She'd gotten her bra and shorts on, but she hadn't zipped them up. He knew what she was going to say before she said it, though. "No."

"*Yes*, Caroline." He began grabbing the rest of her things and shoving them into her bag. They could argue in the car. And, knowing Caroline, they would. "I don't know what kind of man you think I am, but after what's happened between us this weekend, you have to realize that I'm not about to do a damn thing that would put you at risk."

"Except drag me across time zones."

"I'm not leaving you behind, and that's final."

"I'll stay at a hotel," she announced, pulling her shirt over her head.

For a moment, he considered that. Hell, a hotel was where he should have put her in the first place. Anyone else, he would've done just that.

But could he trust that whoever had bugged her house hadn't also bugged her office? That they wouldn't be waiting to track her back to wherever she went—her home, a hotel, the safe house?

Bringing her out here hadn't been his tactical error. Not the big one, anyway.

No, where he'd really screwed up was thinking that he could separate this weekend with her from everything else—his work with the foundation, his job investigating the corruption case, his life. All of it.

He hadn't put the case first. He'd made an exception for Caroline because when he'd looked at her, he'd felt this spark—and the power of that pull had completely erased his professional distance.

She was his assignment. That was all that should be happening between them.

But now that he'd gotten in this deep with her, he couldn't walk away. Or fly away, as the case might be.

"No," he announced.

"Why the hell not?" It was easier to have this argument with her now that she was fully dressed. She grabbed the duffel from him and gave him the kind of look that most likely had wayward attorneys wetting their pants. She was ferocious, his Caroline. "Give me one good reason why, Tom. One really freakin' *good* reason."

He could run through the list of collateral damage this corruption case had left over the years. Lives destroyed, reputations ruined. Justice subverted.

Or he could argue about her personal safety. He could go into excruciating detail about how he'd seen other people's houses get bugged and that information had been used to wreck their lives. He could scare the hell out of her, because a scared witness was willing to do anything to stay safe.

He could also tell her what, up until sixty hours ago, had been the truth—that one person's inconvenience and discomfort meant nothing—not hers, not his. Breaking this case open was the only thing that mattered, and he would do whatever it took to finally get to the bottom of who was buying and blackmailing judges.

He did none of those things. Instead, he closed the distance between them, pulled her into his chest and kissed the holy hell out of her. She tasted of coffee and Caroline, a jolt to his system that he was already addicted to.

"Because," he said when he broke the kiss. Her eyes were closed and she was breathing hard, and if they weren't pushing deadlines, he'd lay her out on the bed and to hell with the rest of the world. "Come with me, Caroline. I..."

He almost said he needed her. Which was *not* true. He needed to know she was safe. He needed to know she was beyond the grasp of blackmailers and violent criminals.

It wasn't like she was someone he couldn't live without.

"Just come with me," he finished, which was not a good reason. It barely qualified as a bad reason, but damn it, it was early and he had to get her to the airport.

Her brow furrowed and her tongue traced the seam of her lips. It was physically painful, resisting the urge to lean down and replace her tongue with his own, but he managed to keep his distance. "Please," he added, way too late.

Her shoulders sagged. "I am *definitely* going to regret this," she murmured as she shouldered her duffel. "What the hell. Let's go to DC. But," she added, jabbing him in the chest with her finger, "you better make it worth it."

"I will," he promised, trying not to grin and failing. "Trust me, I will."

Nine

"Celine. It's me. Listen, there's been a change of plans."

Caroline had no idea if she was supposed to be eavesdropping—but it was hard not to. Tom was pacing in a small circle about five feet away from her. That was all there was room for at the gate in Minneapolis, while they waited for their connecting flight.

But even that small space couldn't contain his energy. Caroline couldn't stop staring at him. Even though she was beyond irritated with the man, there was still something about him that called to her.

Tom's voice was pitched low, and she had to strain to hear him over the noise in the terminal.

She'd had no plans to be in Minneapolis today. Sure, it was always great to come home again, but being stuck at the airport for a ninety-minute layover wasn't exactly a homecoming.

"I'm bringing a guest," Tom went on.

Well. At least Caroline had been upgraded from security risk to guest. That had to count for something, right?

Tom's gaze cut over to her. "For a case…No. Don't worry—she'll be fine. But we might have to change dinner plans."

Caroline was tempted to point out that nothing about this situation was fine, but she didn't want to interrupt. Who was Celine? Not a girlfriend, she was pretty sure. But not a hundred percent sure, because she wasn't one hundred percent sure about any of this. Had she really been pulled onto a plane by the man of her dreams without luggage, toiletries, coffee…?

"We're traveling light, so if you could have something for her tonight?…Yeah. I'm sorry to be such a pain."

Wait. Had Tom Yellow Bird just apologized? Oh, she had to meet this Celine. Because Caroline was reasonably sure she'd never heard the man apologize for anything, and he'd quasi-kidnapped her twice now.

No, he hadn't kidnapped her. That wasn't fair to him. She had, after all, willingly gone along with him both times.

And why had she done that? There wasn't any rational reason for why she had thrown caution, common sense and her professional reputation to the wind. Sure, Tom would try to dress the last four days up as a matter of her safety. Yes, there'd been something off in her house.

But who were they kidding?

She'd come with him because she couldn't help herself. Tom Yellow Bird made her want to do things that she shouldn't—want things she shouldn't. And as ridiculous as this whole situation might be, she'd come with him because it'd meant another few days with him. It'd meant learning a little more about Tom Yellow Bird.

It'd meant another night in his arms and, apparently, that was worth the risk.

A sour feeling settled into her stomach. At this point, at ten fifteen on a Monday morning, when she was supposed to be in court, Caroline was completely out of rational reasons for any of the choices she'd made since calling Tom on Friday night.

It was hard to even remember how this had started—her house had felt wrong. Tom thought it was bugged. Someone was potentially planning to blackmail her.

So what had she done in response to a blackmail threat? Run away with the FBI agent assigned to the case and thrown herself at him. And now she was running away with him again, this time to Washington, DC.

For someone who prided herself on making the right choices ninety-nine out of a hundred times, Caroline was sure screwing things up.

"Hold on, I'll ask her." Tom turned to her. "What size do you wear?"

It wasn't like he hadn't seen her naked and didn't have a really good idea of her weight. So this was just another indignity. "Eight."

Tom repeated the number and then said, "What?… Oh. Yeah, okay." Then he handed the phone to her. "Be polite," he said in a low voice.

She scowled. When was she not polite? "Hello?"

"If you could just give me your dress size, shoe size, hair color, eye color, skin tone and body type, that would make this so much easier," a cultured woman's voice said with no other introduction.

Whoever this was, she certainly sounded like a Celine.

"Excuse me?" Maybe this was some sort of personal assistant? Frankly, at this point, nothing would surprise her.

"For tonight?" Celine said, as if she were speaking to a child. "Thomas has indicated you will need something to wear."

Thomas? She looked up at him. He was frowning, but that could have just been his normal expression at this point. "What's happening tonight?"

Tom's frown deepened. If she hadn't spent the weekend wrapped around him, she might be intimidated.

"Why, the Rutherford Foundation's annual gala benefit," Celine announced, as if that were the most obvious thing in the world instead of a complete surprise. "Thomas is, as usual, the guest of honor. And if he thinks enough of you to bring you as his guest, we can't have you looking like you just walked off the plane, can we?"

The Rutherford Foundation? Later, she was going to strangle the man. Slowly. But she'd promised to be polite—and she had to admit, she desperately wanted to meet the woman Tom not only apologized to freely, but would let call him Thomas. "Oh. Yes. He mentioned something about that," she lied. "I'm a size eight and I wear a seven and a half in shoes."

"Hair color? Eye color? Bra size? Are you pear shaped or top-heavy?"

This was not awkward at all, she kept repeating to herself as she answered the questions. Her face felt like it was on fire with embarrassment, but she answered as honestly as she could.

"Thank you," Celine said, and oddly, she did sound genuinely grateful. "If I could speak with Thomas again? Oh—I didn't even get your name."

"Caroline. Caroline Jennings." Should she mention she was a judge? Or was that on a need-to-know basis? "Thank you for your help," she said, remembering her manners. "Will I have the chance to meet you tonight?"

Celine laughed, a delicate, tinkling sound. "Oh, I wouldn't miss it for the world."

With that vaguely ominous statement, Caroline handed the phone back over. What the hell had she gotten herself into?

This wasn't her world. Her world was predictable and safe. She lived her life to minimize the number of risks she took. Risks like running off with a man who was little more than a stranger, or falling into bed with said stranger.

Or jetting across the country to attend a gala benefit for a foundation with a dress code that required her body shape to be up for analysis, for God's sake.

She was skipping work. That was a hazard to her professional reputation. And Tom…

"We'll see you in a few hours," he told Celine, his gaze cutting over to Caroline.

Tom was definitely hazardous.

Tom ended the call and loomed over her. Unlike in Pierre, where they had been the only people in the airport besides a ticket clerk who'd also been the baggage handler, the Minneapolis Airport was crowded with people. Tom had only been able to snag one seat at their gate, and he had insisted Caroline sit in it.

It was sort of chivalrous. Thoughtful, even—which was quite a change of pace from him waking her up at the butt crack of dawn and informing her she was flying to the nation's capital with him, no discussion allowed. But that one small chivalrous act was barely a drop in an ocean of other things that were the complete opposite of thoughtful.

"We're going to a gala benefit for the Rutherford Foundation?" she asked, wondering if she should pinch herself—hard—to wake up from this strange dream. "You don't think you might have mentioned that before I had to give my body type to some woman named Celine?"

"I wanted to make sure you would be welcomed at the benefit," he said, choosing each word carefully.

She tried to be understanding. Really, she did. If she were to look at the situation objectively, Tom's behavior made perfect sense within a certain context. And that context was that he was a widowed officer of the law. He'd lived alone for years. He was used to giving orders and having them followed. He was used to being right, because who was going to contradict him? The criminals he arrested?

No, she had known from the very first moment Tom had walked into her courtroom that he did things his way, and honestly, that was part of his appeal. Or it had been, until this morning.

But damn it, she was not some common criminal he was shuffling from courthouse to jail. Hell, she wasn't even a witness that he was protecting at all costs. She didn't know what she was, except the woman who couldn't resist doing whatever he told her to.

She was definitely going to regret this.

"For the record," she began, standing so he wasn't staring down at her, "you should have told me first. Even better, you should've asked me to go as your date. It's a lot more effective than ordering me around and keeping me in the dark."

"I'm not—it wasn't—"

"You were and it was," she interrupted. "I like you, Tom. I hope you realize that. I wouldn't be here if I didn't."

He took a breath that looked shaky. "I am aware of that."

God save her from men who couldn't talk about

their feelings. Caroline pressed on. "But if you keep treating me like…like a chess piece you can move around the board whenever the whim strikes you, this won't end well for either of us."

She wasn't ready for what happened next. His scowl slipped, and underneath, she saw… vulnerability. Worry. "You're not a chess piece, Caroline." He stepped in closer to her. She felt him all the way down to her toes. "Not to me."

Her whole body leaned toward him without her express permission. Something more—that's what he was to her. That's what she was to him, right?

No. Get a grip, she ordered herself. She'd rather be mad at him. There was nothing wrong with angry sex, after all. But tenderness was dangerous. For all she knew, affection could be deadly.

So she didn't allow herself to feel any of that. "Good," she said, making sure to keep her voice firm, "Now, why don't you tell me about this gala benefit I'm accompanying you to this evening?"

Celine had done as she'd promised. More than she'd promised, Tom realized when he and Caroline walked into the room at the Watergate Hotel. Celine and Mark always offered to put him up in their guest room, but he'd been staying at this hotel for years. It was better this way. The room was a small apartment, really, with an office, dining room, kitchen and a generous bedroom—with a generous bed.

There, right there in the middle of the room, were boxes from Bloomingdale's, stacked seven high on the coffee table. Hanging over the back of the bedroom door were two garment bags, one long and one shorter.

An unfamiliar twinge of nervousness took him by surprise. He couldn't be nervous. He did this every year. He'd attended enough formal events that he could push through feeling that he was an impostor. He belonged here now.

At first, coming back to DC, getting suited up in his tuxedo and pressing the flesh with the political movers and shakers had almost been more than Tom could bear, but he'd done it to honor Stephanie's memory and pay his respects to her parents.

By now this trip was old hat to him. He was on a first-name basis with those movers and shakers. His custom-made tuxedo was cut to conceal his gun. He could chat with Mark and Celine without feeling like his heart was being ripped out of his chest. There was no reason to be nervous.

"Holy hell." Caroline's voice came from behind him. She sounded stunned. "Look at this place! And—whoa." She stepped around him and stared at the boxes. "How much clothing did she get for me?"

It was a fair question. In addition to the seven boxes on the coffee table, there were three more on the floor. "Knowing Celine, she probably got you a few options, just in case something didn't quite work." A huge clotheshorse, Celine would have enjoyed the opportunity to shop for someone else.

But he didn't say that. He felt out to sea here, because he hadn't had a date, as Caroline had started calling this evening, in…

Okay, he wasn't going to think about how long.

It wasn't a date, though. He was not dragging her around the country just so he could have sex with her whenever he wanted. This was a matter of safety. Of public interest. He couldn't compromise this case any more than he already had.

Yeah, he wasn't buying that, either.

Caroline reached over as if to pick up the top box and then pulled her hand back. "I don't think I can afford what she picked out."

"I'm paying for it." She turned and launched another blistering glare at him. "I'm the one who dragged you out here," he reminded her. "The least I can do is foot the bill for the appropriate evening wear."

She chewed at her lip, and even though his head wasn't a mess and he wasn't nervous about tonight, he wanted to kiss her anxiety away. He wanted to do a lot more than kiss her. He wanted her back in his bed, where they should have been this morning.

"And her husband—that's Senator Rutherford, right?" She nervously twisted her hands together. "I can't believe that he was your father-in-law. And I really can't believe that I'm going to a party with them tonight." Her brow wrinkled as she stared at the boxes.

"You'll do fine," he said—not so much because it was what she needed to hear, although it might be. But it was because he needed to hear it, too.

He was just introducing the only woman he'd slept with since Stephanie to her parents. No big deal.

"We've got a few hours," he said, carrying his

bag into the bedroom. He needed to hang his tux and make sure his shoes were shined. "I need to check in with the office."

The look on her face let him know loud and clear that he'd said the wrong thing. "Oh."

Damn it. He immediately saw his mistake. What kind of jerk was he to drag her to DC and then ignore her? "What I meant to say is, after I check in, if there's something you want to see, we could go do that."

She snorted in what he hoped was amusement, but her face softened and he got the distinctive sense that she knew he was trying. Mostly failing, but trying anyway. "Play tourist with you? Now you're getting the hang of this date thing. Sadly, I don't think we have time to wander the Mall. I need to see what I'm dealing with here—" she gestured to the boxes "—and I definitely need a shower." She looked again at all the boxes. "I hope there's some makeup in there or something."

The mention of a shower caught his attention. Shower sex was definitely one of his fantasies. Nothing in this day had gone according to plan. Yeah, he was rolling with the punches as best he could, but...

He wanted to relieve some of the tension that had started to build the moment she'd sat up in bed this morning, the sheet pooling at her waist.

He wanted to get her naked and wet, their bodies slick and then he wanted...

But he couldn't. He had ignored his responsibilities long enough. He had to do his job. Long after whatever this thing with Caroline was had ended, the job would still be there.

So instead of leading her to the shower and stripping her bare, he took a step back and said, "I'm sure there is. And if there isn't, I'll get you some." She notched an eyebrow at him. "I'll have someone who knows something about makeup get some for you," he corrected. "Deal?"

"Deal." She cracked her knuckles and made for the boxes. "Let's see what we've got."

Ten

What they had, Caroline concluded an hour later, was half a department store's worth of clothes. *Good* clothes. The kind of designer names that made her bank account weep with frustration.

Armani. Gucci. Halston, even. Celine Rutherford had exceptional taste and apparently an unlimited budget.

How on earth was she supposed to let anyone else pay for all of this? Four gowns—gowns!—plus two summery sundresses, a pair of Bermuda shorts, a pair of twill trousers, four different tops to pair with the pants, matching accessories and shoes for every outfit. For God's sake, there was even lingerie in here. Really nice lingerie. The kind a woman wore when she was intent upon seducing a man. Pale pink silk, delicate black lace—damn.

And of course there was makeup. Hell, the stuff in one of those bags wasn't even the brands she sometimes splurged on at the department stores. Tom Ford? Guerlain?

She was looking at a complete wardrobe that had probably set Tom back close to ten thousand dollars. More, if the stones in the necklaces and earrings were real diamonds and emeralds and not reasonable facsimiles. She hoped like hell they were fakes.

Her chest began to tighten as she surveyed the luxury goods. This wasn't right. This was like when she'd been a first-year prosecutor, drowning under the weight of her student loans, and had woken up one day to discover that, somehow, all of her debts had been mysteriously paid off.

It had been a mistake then not to undo that. It would be a mistake now to accept all of this finery.

What complicated things even more was that she was afraid she was falling for Tom. Some of him, anyway. She wasn't in love with the domineering parts of him that gave orders first and made requests second. But a part of her even found that appealing. He was just such a strong man, confident and capable, willing to run toward danger. But underneath that was a streak of vulnerability that tugged at her heartstrings.

Wrap that all up in his intense eyes and hard body and—well, was it any wonder she was in Washington, DC, willing to compromise her morals *again* just to be with him?

She glanced back at the doorway that led to a small office. Tom had disappeared in there when she'd started unpacking the boxes—he obviously wasn't the kind of guy who was heavily invested in women's fashion. Every so often, she could hear him talking—was he working or was he checking in on Maggie?

It almost didn't matter. Caroline strongly suspected that, when it came to his friends, his focus was just as intense as it was when he was working a case. He took his job seriously and she respected the hell out of him for it, even if she selfishly wanted him all to herself.

If this whole crazy weekend turned into something more…what would they even look like as a couple? She couldn't ask him to stop working—it was clearly such a huge part of who he was, just like being a judge was fundamental to who she was. It wouldn't be selfish to ask him to pull him back from his duties to spend more time with her—it would be unconscionable.

A flare of guilt caught her by surprise. No, she couldn't compromise his ability to do his job—any more than she already had. And she couldn't compromise her reputation any more than she already had, either. Gifts as extravagant as this wardrobe looked bad, and when it came to conflicts of interest, appearance was everything.

Which meant she couldn't keep the clothes.

She'd have to wear one of the dresses and the shoes. But she wouldn't take the tags off anything else. The rest of it was all going back.

Now she just had to figure out how to tell Tom that. She didn't want to seem ungrateful, but she didn't want it to look like she could be bought for the price of designer formal wear.

She needed a shower to clear her head. "I'm going to start getting ready," she announced after she tapped on the office door. "Is it okay if I shower first?"

He shot her a look that kicked the temperature of the room up a solid five degrees, and Caroline found herself hoping that he'd offer to join her. Then he said, "Be my guest."

She was not disappointed by this. She needed to shave and exfoliate, and it was hard to do all those things with a man in the tub with her. So this was just fine. Really.

She was rinsing her hair when the door to the bathroom clicked open. She turned to find Tom leaning against the sink, watching her.

There was something about the way he was holding his body that made her nipples tighten in anticipation. Maybe he had come to join her, after all. She shouldn't want him here. She shouldn't willfully keep making the same mistakes, over and over.

But here he was, and she was powerless to send him away.

"Are you waiting on the shower?" As she asked, she ran her fingers over her chest and down her stomach, rinsing the soap off.

Even at this distance—maybe six feet between them—she could see his eyes darken. He practically vibrated—but he didn't move.

"Or," she said, musing out loud, "you could join me. Plenty of room." She made a big show of scooting to one side.

He made a noise that echoed off the tiled walls. His

clothes hit the floor, and the next thing she knew, he had her pinned against the wall, his erection nudging at her. "Did I mention that this is one of my fantasies?"

"Is it, now?" She dug her fingers into his hair, tilting his head back so the water sluiced over him. "I don't recall you mentioning your fantasies. Just mine." It felt dangerous to tease him like this, but God help her, it felt right, too. Somehow, she knew she was safe with him.

"Caroline," he groaned. He flipped her around—and none too gently, either. "I can't wait—I have to have you right now." He nudged her legs apart with his knee and tilted her bottom up. "Okay?"

"Yes," she hissed, arching her back to give him better access.

He was against her and then he thrust inside her in one smooth movement, filling her so effortlessly that she almost screamed from the pleasure of it. But she just managed to keep her noises restrained.

The he wound her hair around his fist and pulled her head back. "You have no idea," he whispered in her ear, his voice hoarse, "*no* idea how much I love hearing you scream." As he spoke, his other hand reached around and took possession of her breast, his fingers expertly finding her nipple and tormenting it mercilessly.

Caroline shimmered as she surrendered to the sensations. Her body adjusted to his and then he began to thrust, long, measured strokes timed with his fingers tugging on her nipple, his hand pulling gently but steadily on her hair and his mouth, his teeth on her neck and shoulders.

This weekend had been intense, a fantasy played out in real time. But this? She flattened her hands against the wall and gave herself up to him completely.

"Scream for me, Caroline," he whispered in her ear, his voice desperate, his hands on her body as he drove into her again and again.

It was all she could do, the only gift she could give him. And she gave it freely. "Tom—*Tom*!"

He growled and sank into her. Caroline's world exploded around her in a shimmering white light. Seconds later, Tom relinquished his hold on her hair and breast and dug his hands into her hips. He slammed into her with a ferocity that she knew she'd never find in another man. A second climax had her screaming his name again as he froze, her name a groan of pleasure on his lips.

They sagged against each other, the wall holding them up. Without warning, Caroline began to laugh. It came from deep inside—a release that she hadn't known she'd needed.

Tom spun her in his arms and tilted her head back. "Okay?" he asked, an amused smirk on his lips.

She was laughing so hard tears ran down her face. All these years and *this* was what she'd been chasing. She'd had a bunch of mediocre sex and occasionally some good sex, all because it was careful. Safe. But this?

She'd always known something was missing. And all it took was one cryptic FBI agent with an overprotective streak and the fantasies she'd nurtured quietly for years to show her how much she'd settled for.

And the hell of it was, she'd *known*. From the first moment she'd caught him staring at her across the courtroom, so caught up in her that he forgot to be seated—she'd known he was something special.

"I've never been better," she said when she finally had herself under control as she pulled him back into her arms. "Never."

"Good," he said against her lips. "Because I have a few more fantasies I want to try out."

She tried to look coy, which was something of a challenge, given that they were naked underneath a stream of water. "Don't we have to go to some gala?"

He cupped her face in his hands. "I'm not talking about just tonight, Caroline."

The full meaning of his words hit her. Dating. A relationship, even. *"Oh."*

His grin was wolfish. How could a man look so hungry when he'd just been sated so spectacularly?

"Let's get through tonight," he told her. "Then..."

"Right. Tonight." She had to put on a gown and what were probably real jewels and hobnob with heiresses and power brokers.

What else did he have in store for her?

She tried on the black dress, but, as expected, she couldn't wear either her serviceable beige bra or the silky strapless pink one Celine had provided. She decided to go with the plum gown. The color was deep and rich, not quite purple and not quite maroon. It wasn't bright enough that she'd stand out in a crowd, but it wasn't black, either.

Although the floor-length dress was sleeveless, it had two little straps that met at the center of the neckline, a V nestled between her breasts that provided just enough support that she wouldn't spend the evening tugging at the top. She paired it with a cuff bracelet that she hoped like hell was covered in rhinestones and not real diamonds. Along with that went sparkly chandelier earrings. She chose the kitten-heeled silver sandals.

She managed to get the dress zipped on her own and then turned to look at her reflection in the full-length mirror on the closet door. What she saw stunned her—was that really her?

Because the woman looking back at her was glamorous—gorgeous, even. That woman bore only a passing resemblance to Caroline.

Maybe she could do this—waltz into this world of power and wealth, and if not fit in, at least fake it for an evening.

"Caroline? We need to leave," Tom called out from the living room.

"Have you heard anything about Maggie?" she yelled back, touching up her lipstick. Not that her lipstick needed to be touched up. It was possible she was stalling.

None of this seemed real. The clothes, the jewelry, being in a DC hotel room with Tom—she was afraid to break the strange spell he'd cast over her.

"They managed to get the contractions stopped and everything is stabilized. They're still keeping her another night, but better safe than sorry at this point."

"Good. I'm glad to hear it." It was obvious Maggie was important to him, but more than that, Caroline didn't wish pregnancy complications on anyone.

Finally, she couldn't stall any longer. She wanted to make a good impression on his…were they still his in-laws? Former in-laws? She didn't know, but she did know it was bad form to keep them waiting.

She took a deep breath and opened the door. "How do I look?"

Tom looked up, and his mouth fell open. Then he dropped his phone and came to his feet.

Her pulse began to beat hard as he took in everything—and as she stared at him in return. Good Lord, he was wearing a tuxedo. Which shouldn't have been a surprise—she'd seen him unpack it, after all. And this was obviously the sort of event where tuxedos were de rigueur.

But the way the tuxedo fit him? Sweet merciful heavens. It was like a tall, dark, handsome James Bond had just walked off the screen and into her hotel room. Tom made a suit look amazing, a pair of jeans even better.

But Tom in a tux was something else entirely. Her nipples went rock hard at the sight, and suddenly, the dress seemed a half size too small.

As if she wasn't nervous enough, a creeping sense of doubt moved up her back. She'd pushed it aside earlier, in the shower. But now reality reared its head.

Tom was still staring, that unmistakable hunger in his eyes. There were so many things she didn't know about him. She knew he'd loved his wife, but had he moved on from her death?

This was not her world. It had been Stephanie's world, and Caroline knew that she could never compete.

He still hadn't said anything yet. She looked down at the dress and shot him a nervous smile. "Is this okay?" She did a little turn so he had full view of the dress in the back.

When she got turned around again, he was giving her such a hard look she recoiled back a step. "Tom? Is it all right?"

"Good," he said, his voice tight.

She began to panic. She'd thought this gown was the best option, but maybe it didn't make her look as glamorous as she'd thought. "I've never been to a gala benefit for a foundation before. There were other dresses..."

"No," he cut her off. "That one's perfect. You look amazing."

She blinked at him. "Was that a compliment?"

The look of confusion on his face almost undid her right then and there. "Was it?"

This man. "No, the correct answer is, of course it was."

She gave him a long look and she'd swear the room brightened when the lightbulb went off over his head. "Of course it was. You look amazing, Caroline."

Even though she'd had to walk him up to the words, the sincerity in his voice made her cheeks warm. "Okay, good. Everything else can be returned—except for the makeup and..." She looked down at the dress. She didn't want to discuss the lingerie with him right now.

That seemed like a bad idea because they had to be someplace very soon and she suspected that, if she brought panties into the discussion, she'd find herself removing them within seconds. "Everything I'm wearing right now. It's far too much money for me to casually accept the rest as a gift. I don't want to create the appearance of impropriety."

His eyes crinkled, and she got the feeling he was trying not to laugh at her, because there was nothing proper about any of this, appearances or otherwise, and they both knew it.

"Caroline," he said and suddenly he was looking at her with undisguised hunger, his voice the sound of sex on the wind, "try not to think like a lawyer tonight, all right? This is a date, not a court hearing. You look amazing."

She was many things—intelligent, competent, dedicated—but so very rarely was she *desirable*. Or glamorous. And right now, she was both.

She was keeping this dress.

He was the most dangerous man she had ever met. Not because he had the capacity to be deadly or because he filled out that tuxedo.

It was because of the way he made her feel. Glamorous and desirable—those were terrifying emotions. They made her do unpredictable things, like skip work and crash a gala. Worse, she was afraid of what would happen if they were combined with other emotions—tenderness, affection and who could forget sexual satisfaction? All those things swirled around inside her until they formed a superstorm of something that felt much stronger than infatuation, more potentially damaging than a hurricane.

She had once fancied herself in love. With Robby, of course. Looking back now, she couldn't remember what, exactly, she had loved about him. She didn't recall him being a particularly good student, nor was he exceptionally kind to small animals. He was just… there. He'd liked her, for whatever reason. She'd been young. Being liked was half the battle.

She liked to think she wasn't stupid anymore. And she definitely wasn't young.

So this wouldn't be the same thing she'd had with Robby. She was older and wiser. Tom had hinted that they'd have something more after this weekend—but there was no law that it had to be marriage. They could keep doing this—having a consensual, satisfying relationship that didn't involve messy emotions or the potential for heartache. She should keep some distance between them and cling to the safety it provided.

Yes, that's what she should do. But what she did instead was sashay toward him, her hips swaying seductively. "Tom…"

He looked at her with such longing that she wondered how late they could be. But then he said, "We should go."

She wasn't disappointed at that. Not even a little. "We should."

But after this little gala, they were coming back here. And in the morning, she wasn't leaving until she'd found out how far he was willing to take this.

Eleven

"Nervous?"

Caroline rolled her eyes at Tom. "No, why would I be nervous? I'm just wearing a gown and accessories worth thousands of dollars, after riding in a limo far nicer than the one I took to high school prom, next to an armed man wearing a tuxedo, on my way to meet your former in-laws, who happen to be insanely wealthy and also powerful, all while attending a gala benefit filled with the elite in honor of your late wife. Why would I be nervous?"

The corner of his mouth ticked up, but he didn't smile. He couldn't, not with her on his arm as they made their way into the crush of the annual Rutherford Foundation Gala Benefit and Ball. When she'd walked out of the bedroom in that dress, the fabric clinging to her every curve, he'd been stunned past the point of coherence, physically shaking with the effort it took to restrain himself from mussing up her hair and peeling that dress from her body.

He hadn't, because Mark and Celine Rutherford were waiting on them. He had to keep up appearances.

He freakin' hated appearances.

He didn't get nervous anymore—but at times like these, he couldn't help flashing back to the first time Carlson had dragged him along to one of these events. Or the second time. Hell, even the tenth time, he'd still been painfully aware that he didn't belong. It'd gotten better after he'd married Stephanie, but…

But Stephanie, God rest her soul, wasn't on his arm. He didn't have her social graces smoothing the way and making sure he fit in.

Instead, Caroline was with him.

And there was no turning back.

He remembered how, the first few times they'd attended a function together, Stephanie had kept up a steady stream of survival tips, designed to put him at ease. So he did the same for Caroline. "It's open bar. But I'd recommend going easy on champagne."

"If it's all the same to you, I'd like to avoid making a complete and total fool of myself in front of—how many members of Congress will be here?"

"Probably no more than thirty. Or did you want to include former senators and congressmen?"

She stumbled, but he steadied her. Once she had her balance back, she whispered, "I can't tell if you're being serious or if you're teasing."

He was definitely teasing her. "Don't panic. There probably won't be more than two Supreme Court justices in attendance."

She hit him with her clutch. Hard. "Later, I'm going to get even with you."

He damn near grabbed her and marched her right back out to the limo. They didn't even have to make it to the hotel—the limo was big and had an abundance of flat surfaces. He'd wrinkle her dress with wild abandon before he peeled it right off her luscious body.

But he didn't. Instead, he kissed her hand, his lips warm against her knuckles. "Caroline."

She took a deep breath that did some very interesting things to her cleavage, but then she turned her gaze up to his face. Her eyes were so full of hope and affection that suddenly his own breath caught in his chest. "Yes?"

Yeah, he'd been trying to convince himself he'd brought her here for noble reasons. But now? After he'd taken her in the shower? Moments before he introduced her to the Rutherfords?

He realized how damn wrong he'd been. The case wasn't the reason they were here. Her security wasn't why she was wearing that gown, nor why he was about to introduce her to the Rutherfords.

She was the reason. He hadn't been able to put her in a hotel and forget about her. He hadn't been able to leave her behind.

He wasn't sure he could.

"I'm glad you're here with me."

She gasped, a delicate blush on her cheeks, and he

felt himself leaning toward her. The rest of the crowd fell away, and it was just him and her and this spark that had always existed between them.

Just then, he heard, "Thomas!" The sound of Celine Rutherford's voice snapped him out of his insanity.

Celine swanned toward him, glamorous as usual in a lacy evening gown that managed to make her look at least twenty years younger than she actually was.

"Celine," he said, bending over to kiss her cheek. "You look lovelier than ever."

She did. He braced himself for the pain of seeing her again but it didn't come. Not in the almost overwhelming waves that usually left him dazed, anyway. A dull ache radiated from his chest, but it wasn't as bad as it normally was. Manageable, even.

"You sweet talker, you." Celine beamed, playfully patting his arm.

Tom grinned good-naturedly. "My apologies for being late. I always forget there's traffic here."

She waved this away. "The important thing is that you're here now. You look wonderful, Thomas."

Beside him, Tom was pretty sure he heard Caroline snort in what he hoped was amusement. And he knew why, too. No one called him Thomas for very long.

Except for the Rutherfords. "Celine, may I present Judge Caroline Jennings? She's my guest this evening."

Caroline stepped forward, looking starstruck. "It's a pleasure to meet you, Mrs. Rutherford. I cannot thank you enough for going to all the trouble of pulling that wonderful selection of clothing for me. I hope this meets your specifications?" she asked in a rush, as if the dress Tom had not been able to stop staring at for the last forty minutes was a feed sack on her.

Celine laughed, a light sound. "I think you made the right choice. You look marvelous, dear. That color suits you perfectly."

For years, seeing Celine Rutherford had been the most painful thing Tom had to survive. Stakeouts and violent criminals and occasional shoot-outs—he'd take those any day of the week compared to the mental torture of his annual visit to the Rutherfords. It was easier now, because Stephanie was forever fixed in his mind at twenty-seven years old and Celine got a little older and a little grander every year.

But it still hurt. There was a small, selfish part of him that wished the Rutherfords weren't so kind to him, that they could all let the relationship drift away and Tom wouldn't have to face these memories on a regular basis.

Normally, he would get through this evening by drinking more champagne than was healthy and finding a few other people from the FBI he could talk shop with.

This time? He didn't want to deal with questions about who Caroline was and why she was here. It was bad enough that he was introducing her to Celine.

What the hell was he doing here? There wasn't supposed to be anything between him and Caroline, beyond her role in an ongoing investigation.

But had that stopped him from bringing her to

DC? Or introducing her to his in-laws? Or thinking about a relationship after this?

Nope. All those things he shouldn't be doing, he was doing them anyway. Just to keep her closer.

Celine went on, "And it was no trouble at all. I had so much fun putting the outfits together. I so miss shopping for Stephanie." Her voice trailed off and her eyes got suspiciously shiny. "But then, I suppose I always shall. I do try to keep her spirit alive. This was her foundation, you know. She started it with her trust fund money. Thomas and I keep it going to honor her memory."

"I've always admired what the Rutherford Foundation does," Caroline said, and oddly, she sounded serious about it. "I don't think Tom knows this, but I've actually donated a fair amount of money to the Rutherford Foundation over the years. I admire your objectives about educating girls and women around the world."

"You have?" Celine smiled broadly, any lingering remnants of grief vanished from her eyes. "Why, that's wonderful! It's always a pleasure to meet people who appreciate what we're doing—isn't it, Thomas?"

"It is," he said, staring at Caroline with curiosity. "Why didn't you tell me that?"

She lifted an eyebrow. "I prefer surprising you."

"Oh, I can see we're going to get along famously," Celine said, linking her arm with Caroline's and pulling her away from Tom. "Thomas needs someone who can keep him on his toes. Come, I must introduce you to everyone. Thomas?" she called over her shoulder. "Are you joining us?"

For a long second, he couldn't move. He couldn't talk, even. All he could do was look at Celine and Caroline fast becoming friends and trail along behind the two women, shadowing them like a bodyguard. He was fine. It was just the shock of seeing Celine give what looked a lot like a seal of approval to Caroline. That was throwing him for a loop. Every few feet they paused and greeted someone. Celine introduced Caroline as if they were the oldest of friends.

What would Stephanie think of this? Would she have laughed at him because, as usual, he was taking everything too seriously? Would she have been hurt that Tom was bringing another woman to Stephanie's event? It wasn't like Caroline was replacing anyone. She and Stephanie didn't look alike, didn't have the same sense of humor and definitely didn't have the same background.

All they had in common—besides the ability to fill out an evening gown—was that, for some inexplicable reason, they both cared for Tom.

And he cared for them.

Caroline laughed at something Celine said to Representative Jenkins, and Celine beamed at her. Celine liked Caroline.

Caroline kept him on his toes and didn't let him get away with anything. Even when he steamrolled her, she didn't simper or whine. She gave as good as she got, and he loved it when she did.

Stephanie would've loved Caroline. The realization made his chest tighten.

Mark Rutherford fell into step next to him. "Tom,"

he said, giving Tom a strong handshake. "Good to see you."

"Mark," Tom said. He nodded to where Celine was showing Caroline off. "I would introduce you, but Celine has already staked her territory."

Tom liked his in-laws—he always had. They had never made him feel like he was a dirt-poor Indian who didn't belong. Even if that's what he had been, once upon a time. Tom wondered if they'd approved of Stephanie marrying him, but he'd never know. They had always treated him with warmth and respect.

Mark had aged quite a bit since Stephanie's death. He and his daughter had always been close. His hair had gone almost white within the year, and he had not sought reelection after his term finished in the Senate. His appearance was just another reminder of how much time had actually passed.

"How have you been?" Tom asked.

"Getting by. I'll be glad when this fund-raiser is over. It consumes Celine for months on end. And you know how she is when she gets focused on something." They shared a laugh, but Tom couldn't help looking at Celine and Caroline, who were continuing to make new friends. He knew exactly how his mother-in-law was when she focused on something—and right now, Caroline was the beneficiary of that focus.

"I'm sorry this is awkward," he began, because it felt awkward to him. "But it was unavoidable."

Mark waved this away. "No need to explain. We're thrilled to meet her."

Tom was so focused on Celine and Caroline that

he almost missed what Mark had said—and put it together with something Celine had said earlier—about how Tom needed her to keep him on his toes.

Oh, *no*. Yeah, he'd been thinking about keeping Caroline closer—but he didn't know what that meant right now. It didn't mean wedding bells and babies, that was for sure—and he couldn't have the Rutherfords jumping to that conclusion. He needed to nip this in the bud. "I'm not here *with* Caroline."

Mark gave him a look that Tom had seen many times over the years, one that always made Tom squirm. "Am I reading this wrong? You show up with a gorgeous woman you can't stop staring at and I'm supposed to believe you two aren't involved?"

"She's part of a case." To his own ears, Tom sounded defensive. "You know how important my work is," Tom went on. "The job's not done."

True, none of that had exactly stopped Tom from sleeping with Caroline. Nor had it prevented him from bringing her here. Or telling her he wanted to see her after this trip, too.

His stomach felt like a lead balloon. It'd been one thing when they'd been tucked away in his house or at the hotel, far from prying eyes. But he hadn't been able to leave their relationship there. He'd convinced himself that it was all right—no, vital—to bring Caroline to this party and introduce her to the Rutherfords. And it was a lie. A selfish, willful lie just because he couldn't bear to leave her at a damned hotel in South Dakota.

What had he done? Celine and now Mark were

both taken with Caroline. They were welcoming her into their world with open arms. Tom realized he was setting the Rutherfords up for more heartbreak when this...*thing*, whatever it was with Caroline, ended. He couldn't bear to hurt his in-laws. They'd already lost their daughter.

But more than that, Tom had essentially announced to the whole world that she was important to him when he was supposed to be hiding her, keeping things quiet. He was supposed to be protecting her, and instead, he'd opened them both up to more scrutiny. If someone were looking for something to use against either of them, Tom had just handed it to them on a silver platter.

This was too much. He'd left himself exposed and that made Caroline vulnerable. Hell, it made Celine and Mark vulnerable, too.

What *had* he done?

Mark's eyes sparkled with humor. "I've known you a long time, Tom. I've watched you force yourself to attend these things year after year when it's obvious you'd rather be anywhere else. And I've watched women flirt shamelessly with you." He clapped Tom on the shoulder and chuckled. "You could've had your pick, but they've all been invisible to you. But her?" he said with a nod of his head to where Caroline was laughing at something the House minority whip was saying, "You *see* her. Tell me, is that more important than a job?" Sadness stole over his face again. "It's not. Trust me on this one."

Tom gaped at the man, fighting a rising tide of

indignation. "I was married to your daughter, sir. I loved her."

Mark looked at him with a mixture of kindness and pity. "And she died. We'll never forget her—she's the reason we're all here. But we moved on." He leaned in close, kindness radiating from him. "Maybe you should, too."

Twelve

"I can't believe I met the Speaker of the House!" Caroline marveled as she collapsed back in the seat of the limo. The whole evening had an air of the unreal about it.

Celine Rutherford had—well, she'd worked miracles. Caroline had felt perfectly dressed—because Celine had gone shopping. Caroline had met seemingly every mover and shaker in Washington, DC—because Celine introduced her.

And then there was Tom—who was currently sitting silently on the other side of the limo, staring out the window as the lights of DC went zipping past. He seemed…lost.

If she'd thought she'd understood that he was the strong, silent alpha male—then this evening had blown that image out of the water. He'd made the rounds by her side, smiling broadly and making small talk like a pro.

Now that the high of hobnobbing with the rich and famous was wearing off, she was acutely aware that she'd been awake since before dawn, had taken two connecting flights and socialized in a high-stress situation.

Still, she reached over and laced her fingers with Tom's. This was not how she'd planned to spend her day, but she was glad she'd come. "I had a wonderful evening. Celine and Mark were a delight."

At one point, she'd seen Mark Rutherford put his arm around Tom's shoulder in a fatherly manner.

But more than that, he'd spoken warmly with his in-laws—it was obvious that he cared for the Rutherfords a great deal, and they obviously thought the world of him.

It was the sort of loving relationship she'd lost when her parents had passed.

Tom had lost so much. She was glad he had the Rutherfords. He needed more people who cared about him in his life. It bothered her to think of him feeling as alone as she sometimes had after her parents' death.

She was being maudlin—which was probably just due to the exhaustion. It had been a long day, after all.

Tom might suck at talking about his feelings, but his actions spoke for him. It was one more piece to the puzzle that made up Tom Yellow Bird.

Dangerous FBI agent. Reserved private citizen. Thoughtful former son-in-law.

Incredibly hot lover.

Somehow, it all came together into a man she couldn't help but be drawn to. Ever since she'd first seen him in her courtroom, she'd felt something between them, and that something was only getting stronger.

"I'm glad to hear this evening wasn't too hard for you."

There was something in his smile, in his tone that gave her pause. "Was it for you?"

He shrugged, as if his pain were no big deal. "No matter how many times I do this, I still don't belong."

She gaped at him in shock. He'd blended in seamlessly while she'd struggled not to be starstruck. How could he possibly think he hadn't belonged?

"But you do," she told him. "Celine and Mark—they adore you, and you obviously care for them, too. You fit in better than I did." If it hadn't been for Celine, Caroline would have been hiding in the corner with a glass of wine, too anxious to brave the crowd.

He pinned her with his gaze—one she'd seen before. It was the same look he'd given the defendant in the court case—the day she'd met him.

Her back automatically stiffened. Why was he glaring at her? But then, just underneath that stone-cold exterior, she glimpsed something else—something vulnerable.

Scared, she thought as he began to speak. "Do you know where I came from?" he demanded, his voice quiet. It still carried in the limo. "Do you have *any* idea?"

She blinked in confusion. "You said… I thought… the reservation that's less than thirty miles from your house?"

"Yes, but that doesn't tell you where I'm from. Because I *don't* belong here." His scowl deepened. If she didn't know him like she did, she might have been afraid.

But she wasn't. "The Red Creek tribe is pretty small—fewer than four thousand people. I grew up on the banks of the Red Creek curve in a little…" He looked out the window, but not before she caught a flash of pain on his face. "My town was about four hundred people. We didn't even have a gas station. We had electricity at my house, but we pulled our water from the river."

She could tell that admission had cost him something. He was such a proud man—but he'd grown up in what sounded like very poor circumstances.

How many people knew this about him? His late wife, for sure—but did the Rutherfords know? Any of those people who had been so happy to shake his hand tonight?

She sure as hell wouldn't have guessed it—not from his slick suits and his muscle cars and that cabin that had the finest money could buy, because quality was always worth it.

Why was he telling her this? Was he trying to scare her off—or convince himself that he still didn't belong? "We were all scraping by on government surplus foods," he went on, as if being poor was somehow a character flaw. "The only way to change your fate was to get off the res—so that's what I did. I decided to be an FBI agent—don't ask why. I have no clue where I got the idea."

As he spoke, she could hear something different in his voice for the first time. There was an accent there, something new in the way he clipped his vowels. It was the prettiest thing she'd ever heard.

She smiled, trying to imagine Tom Yellow Bird as a kid. All she got was a shorter guy in a great suit. "But you actually did it," she said softly, hoping to draw him out.

"I did. I got a college scholarship, got my degree in criminal justice and headed for DC. It was this huge city," he added, sounding impossibly young. "I'd never been anywhere bigger than Rapid City, and suddenly there were cars everywhere and people and they were all wearing nice suits—it was *crazy*. If I hadn't had Rosebud and, through her, Carlson—I honestly don't know if I could've made it."

"It was that big of a culture shock?"

"Bigger. I was used to the way people on the reservation treated me—as someone to be proud of. I was an athlete and I was smart enough to get a scholarship. I was a big fish in a very small pond, but DC—that was the whole ocean and it was filled with sharks. And I..." He shook his head and she could feel some of his tension fading away. "I was nothing to them. With this last name? Nothing but a curiosity."

She tried to picture it. After all, she was from

Rochester, Minnesota, originally—and that was a lot smaller than Minneapolis. But she had been a girl moving from a mostly white town to an even larger mostly white town. People never looked at her as a curiosity, because she blended in.

No, she couldn't imagine what it would've been like to go from living on government surplus cheese to being invited to bigwigs' parties in DC because your friend thought it would be fun.

She thought about Tom's house, how it was off the grid but still in the lap of luxury. He squeezed her hand, which she took as a good sign.

Had something happened at the party to upset him? Or was it just seeing his in-laws? She didn't know.

"Is it still like that on the reservation?"

"A few years ago they built a hydroelectric dam. The tribe owns forty percent of it and they used a lot of local labor in the construction. The res still isn't a wealthy place, but it's better. Ask Rosebud about that when you meet her—it's her story to tell."

Caroline blushed from the tips of her toes to her hair, because he'd again, just casually, tossed off the fact that she *would* be meeting one of his oldest friends. That she'd be part of his life moving forward.

Which was what he'd said in the shower, too. But...

She wanted to spend time with him. But she couldn't keep doing what they'd been doing—running away together and ignoring the real world. The last three and a half days had been risky and dangerous and if she kept up this sort of behavior, it might well come back to haunt her.

Still, she wanted to meet his friends. She had the feeling it was another piece to the puzzle that was Tom Yellow Bird. "I'll do that." She was trying to hear what he wasn't saying, because if she knew anything about Tom, it was that what he didn't say was almost as important as what he did. "Have *you* changed the reservation for the better?"

"I try," he went on. "I honor Stephanie by keeping most of her money in the Rutherford Foundation. I have the safe house I told you about. I also fund a bunch of college scholarships. If there's a kid who wants to work hard enough to get off the res, I'm going to help them do it. And no," he added before Caroline could ask the obvious question, "it's not all her money. I invested wisely. It's amazing how easy it is to make money when you already have it," he added in a faraway voice. "Simply *amazing*."

She knew how damned hard it was to start from nothing, to be buried under such debt that a person couldn't breathe, couldn't sleep. "I don't know many FBI agents who run charities. You could have retired, you know."

"The job wasn't done. It still isn't." Something about the way he said that sent a shiver down her spine. "Besides, I don't run the charities. I pay people to run them for me."

"Are any of those people members of the Red Creek tribe?"

His lips curved into a smile that was so very tempting. "Maybe."

And that, more than anything else, was why she was in this car with Tom Yellow Bird. He was just so damned honorable. Yes, he was gorgeous and financially independent—but there was more to him than that.

She had a momentary flash of guilt. He was protecting his people and fighting for what was right. Hell, he was protecting her. He was protecting her and sweeping her off her feet, and she wasn't worthy of him. Because she couldn't make the same claim to being honorable.

She had done her best to make up for her grand mistakes—but a mistake was something you did accidentally. That was the definition of her pregnancy scare, sure. But more likely it was a mistake she'd made by being involved with Robby, by not taking the proper precautions. And after that scare, she'd buckled down. No more Robby; no more casual attitudes about birth control. From then on, she was careful, and it'd paid off. She hadn't experienced that kind of heart-stopping terror again.

But her pregnancy scare was a world of difference from what had happened with the Verango case. There had been nothing noble about her actions, and what she'd done was exactly the sort of thing someone might use against her.

She came *this* close to telling Tom about it. After all, he'd opened up to her. They were moving into uncharted territory here. How easy would it be to say, *I did a favor for a friend and my debts were paid off in full*? One sentence. Less than twenty words. It wasn't like she'd accepted a bribe intentionally—her law professor had manipulated her. But she hadn't returned the money because she hadn't known how.

Instead, she'd made donations—once she had a salary—to charitable causes, including the Rutherford Foundation. By her rough estimates, she'd given away slightly more than the original amount of the loans that had been paid off with dirty money.

"I don't talk about that. About any of that," Tom said, sounding more like himself. "It's…"

If he was trying to convince her that his hardscrabble life and his wife's death were things he should somehow be ashamed of, she was going to kick his butt. "It's brave and honest and true, Tom. To take something like losing your wife and turn it into something good? Not even good—amazing?" Tears pricked at her eyes, and she cupped his cheek. "You are the best man I've *ever* known."

He slid his arm around her shoulder and touched his forehead against hers and said, "It was different tonight. And that was because of you."

Her confession died on her lips. Whatever this was between them, it was good. She cared for him and he cared for her, and there was that something between them that neither of them could deny. This wasn't pretend. This was real.

If she told him about her one mistake, would he

still look at her with that tenderness, with that hunger? Or would he see nothing but a criminal?

The most she could hope for was that no one would put her student loans and Vincent Verango's plea deal together. It was perfectly reasonable that a first-year prosecutor would offer a plea deal to a supposed first-time offender.

"Caroline…" His voice was barely a whisper. "I…"

Yes, she wanted to say. He'd taken her to his house, brought her to Washington. He'd taken her to a gala benefit and introduced her to his late wife's parents. He'd made crazy, passionate love to her. He'd said he wanted to see her after tonight. She'd cast aside common sense to follow him, because there was something between them that was real and true.

Whatever he wanted, the answer was *yes*.

Suddenly, he pulled back, all the way to the other side of the limo. It hurt worse than a slap to the face. "After we get back tomorrow, I'll sweep your house myself."

Maybe that was supposed to be a tender gesture from a man who had forgotten how to discuss emotions. *When you care enough to sweep the house yourself*, she mused.

But there was no missing the way Tom had pulled away—not just physically, but emotionally. Caroline swore she could feel a wall going up around him. "When will I see you again?"

The silence stretched until she was at her breaking point. "We have to be careful to avoid the appearance of impropriety," he finally said.

He wasn't so much throwing her words back at her as using them as laser-guided weapons, because they hit her with military precision. "Oh. Right."

Objectively, she knew this was true. She'd fallen into bed with him this weekend. She'd skipped work today—and tomorrow—by claiming she had the flu. She was wearing ungodly expensive clothing and jewelry that he'd paid for. She was taking stupid risks with her heart, her health and her career. She hadn't had this much sex in years.

If someone really were looking to blackmail her, this weekend would be a great place to start.

So, yes, she knew they needed to put some distance between them. It just made rational sense.

But there'd been that promise of something more in the shower today. She'd started to believe that this wasn't just a crazy weekend—that this was the start of a relationship.

That explained why Tom's mixed signals hurt so much.

"I have to put the job first," he went on, not making it any better. "My feelings for you..."

Hey, at least he had feelings he was admitting to. That had to count for something. "No, I understand. We both have jobs to do. I just...forgot about that for a little while."

Maybe it was just her, but she thought he visibly sagged in relief. "It's easy to forget everything when I'm with you. But when we're back in Pierre..."

Yeah. When she went back to being Judge Jennings and he went back to being Agent Yellow Bird, neither of them would forget.

Damn it all.

Thirteen

"Fourteen." Tom flung the small bag of recording devices onto James Carlson's desk. "Fourteen damn cameras in her home."

It took a lot to piss Tom off. He'd been doing this for a long time. He'd thought that his rage had burned out of him in the years after Stephanie's death.

Apparently, he'd been wrong.

Carlson looked up at him, eyebrows quirked. "That does seem a little excessive."

"A *little*? There were two cameras in her bathroom—one in the shower and one guaranteed to get an up-skirt shot on the toilet. And three in her bedroom! You and I both know the only reason you would need three separate angles of her bed was if someone was planning on mixing footage."

Several years ago, Rosebud Donnelly had been secretly filmed with her husband, Dan, and the tape had been used in an attempt to blackmail Rosebud into dropping a lawsuit against an energy company. She had come to Carlson and Tom for help.

One minute of Rosebud having her privacy violated and her dignity assaulted. It had been a trade-off then because Carlson and Tom had thought—after all these years—that they'd finally found the man behind the curtain, as Tom thought of him. Dan Armstrong's uncle Cecil was an evil man. For years he'd been blackmailing people and paying off judges—including the judge who had made a mockery of the judicial system by using Maggie so very wrongly.

That should have been the end of the case. If this were a movie, it would've been. But it wasn't. Fourteen cameras made it loud and clear—this wasn't over by a long shot.

Why wasn't it over?

Tom sat in the chair in front of James's desk, vibrating with anger. He was capable of violence, but he rarely resorted to it. However, right now? Yeah, right now he could shoot someone. Repeatedly.

What would've happened if he had let Caroline convince herself that she was imagining things? What would've happened if he had left her alone all weekend? If he'd dropped her off Monday morning and gone on his merry way to DC alone?

He'd been right to take her with him. Fourteen cameras proved that. But he'd also been so, so wrong to do so, because he'd still put her in a position of risk.

"You seem a little worked up about this," Carlson said casually, picking up the bag. "What did Judge Jennings say when you told her how many cameras you found?"

"I didn't. I mean, I haven't—yet." He wasn't sure he could bring himself to tell her, because he knew what it would do to her. It would destroy her sense of peace. She wouldn't be able to sleep, to shower—to do anything personal and intimate.

Like this weekend. When she'd stripped and floated in his spring-fed pool under the fading sunlight. Or when she had straddled him and ridden him hard, crying out his name. Or in DC, when he'd paid God only knew how much to outfit her in gowns and jewels so he could introduce her to his in-laws. Or when he'd taken her in the shower.

If he told her about the cameras, she wouldn't be able to be herself. He would take that freedom away from her.

He wasn't sure when he realized that Carlson wasn't talking. It could've been seconds later, it could've been minutes. He looked up to find one of his oldest friends staring at him. Anyone else and Tom might've been able to keep his cards close to his vest. But Carlson was no idiot, and they knew each other too well.

Tom dropped his head into his hands, struggling to find some equilibrium—or at least a little objectivity. But he didn't have any. He hadn't since he'd heard her voice on his phone on Friday, small and afraid.

Hell, who was he kidding? He hadn't had any objectivity when it came to Caroline Jennings since she had walked into that courtroom. And after the last four days, he couldn't even pretend there was distance between them. Because there wasn't. He had been inside her, for God's sake.

"Do you ever think about her?" he heard himself ask. "Stephanie?"

"I do. She was a good woman."

Silence.

Normally, silence would not work on Tom. Waiting was what he did best. In the grand scheme of things, what was a few minutes when someone was hoping to make him slip up?

What was almost ten years without his wife—without anyone?

"Do you think..." He swallowed, calling up the image of Stephanie at that last party, her body wrapped in a silky blue cocktail dress and her mother's sapphires. Stephanie, telling him she was tired and ready to go. Stephanie, smiling indulgently when he said he had just a little more business to see to—he'd catch a cab. She should take the car. The car *her* money had paid for, not his.

Stephanie kissing him goodbye—not on the lips, but on the cheek. Stephanie, walking away from him for the very last time.

He had loved his wife with every bit of his heart and soul. But in the end, he'd only known her for four years. It hadn't been enough. It would never be enough.

In the end, he'd put the job ahead of her. He should have been with her and he hadn't been, because he'd been chasing a lead, hoping for someone to slip up under the influence of alcohol.

Had it been worth it? Tom couldn't even remember what that case had been. He hadn't finished it, he was sure. He'd been lost in burying his wife.

No. The job hadn't been worth it. Maybe it never would be. Wasn't that what Mark Rutherford had said?

"She would've wanted you to move on." Tom looked up and realized that Carlson was no longer sitting behind his desk. He was now leaning against the front of it, looking at Tom with undisguised worry in his eyes. "It's been almost ten years, Tom."

Mark's words, almost exactly. Tom let out a bitter laugh, because it was that or cry, and he didn't cry. Not ever. "It's not like I've been moping. I've been busy."

Carlson smiled indulgently. "That you have. But can you really do this forever?"

"I'll do it until it's finished." Yes, it was easier to think about the job—corruption, the people who were hurt by faceless men of evil.

"No one questions your commitment to this case."

Tom collapsed back into the chair, defeated. "I took her out to the cabin. And then I took her to DC with me. I introduced her to Celine and Mark. There. Happy now?"

It was difficult to shock Carlson, but in that moment, Tom was pretty sure he had succeeded. He knew for certain when Carlson said, "No shit."

"It might have been a mistake," he conceded—which was an understatement, to be sure. Because before Caroline had called him, fear in her voice, Tom had been content to watch her from a distance. But now?

No distance. None. Which was why he'd practically begged for distance that night in DC. It had hurt like hell to push her away, but it'd been the right thing to do. This proved it.

He glanced back at Carlson, and if he didn't know better, he would say his friend was trying not to laugh. And if Carlson laughed, Tom was going to punch him. It would feel good to punch someone right about now.

"I've got to meet this woman. Maggie will love her."

Tom groaned. This was only getting worse. "I might have compromised the case." Because he had definitely compromised Caroline Jennings. Repeatedly.

Carlson did burst out laughing. "Right, because I've never done anything—including sleeping with a witness—that might have compromised a case. Or do you not remember how I met my wife?" Carlson actually *hooted*, which was not a dignified noise. Tears streamed down his cheeks. "Damn, man—you've been an FBI agent for too long. There's more to life than arresting the next bad guy, Tom." He leaned over and picked up a picture of Maggie. He had several scattered around the office, but this one was newer—a soft-focus shot of her in the hazy afternoon sunlight, cradling her pregnant belly. "So much more."

Tom worked real hard not to be jealous of his

friends' happiness, but he was having a moment of what could reasonably be described as weakness, and in that moment, he was green with envy. "Be that as it may, I'm not going to continually compromise this case. Someone sent her flowers. Someone bugged her house. I'm going to go sweep her office after this, but I'm not going to be shocked if it's bugged, too. Sooner or later, someone's going to reach out to her."

Carlson looked at him for a moment before silently agreeing to go along with the subject change. "Do they have anything on her?"

Tom shook his head. "She's so clean she squeaks. I think that's why they resorted to the cameras—there's nothing else to blackmail her with." Except for how he'd flown her across the country and showered her with gowns and jewels and…

"We need her," Carlson said, any friendliness gone from his voice. "If they reach out to her, I want her to play along and see how much information she can get before they become suspicious. This could be a game changer, Tom."

Carlson wasn't just stating an obvious fact—he was reminding Tom to keep his pants zipped from here on out.

He stood, knowing what he had to do and knowing how damned hard it was going to be.

He wanted her. But that need scared him—because it endangered her, of course. His wants and needs had nothing to do with this. Not a damn thing. The only thing that mattered was that he couldn't risk her. "I need to keep an eye on her, do regular sweeps of her house and office. But I'll do anything to keep her safe between now and then. Including not seeing her."

Carlson considered this. "Does she mean that much to you?"

If it were anyone else but Carlson, he'd lie. And Tom hated lying. But Carlson was one of his oldest friends, and he owed the man nothing less than the truth. "She does."

"Well, then," Carlson said, pushing off the desk and resting a hand on Tom's shoulder. "You do what you need to do."

Tom nodded and turned to go. But when his hand was on the doorknob, Carlson spoke again. "She would've wanted you to be happy, Tom. You know that, right?"

It was like a knife in the back. Tom opened the door and walked out without responding.

Fourteen

Caroline did her best to go back to normal, but it wasn't easy. The trip left her drained in ways she hadn't expected. Apparently getting up at crazy hours and jetting across the country was exhausting.

But that minor inconvenience wasn't the only problem.

Where the hell was Tom Yellow Bird? He was like a ghost in her life. She hadn't seen him in the weeks since they'd come back from DC, but she got regular text messages from him that included the date, time and location he'd swept for bugs. He apparently had checked her office and her house on alternating days—but never while she was there. And he didn't tell her if he'd found anything, just that her house was clean now.

Not that she needed a text to know he'd been in her home. Just like she'd felt it when someone had broken in several weeks ago, she could feel Tom's presence. It was unnerving how easily she could tell that he'd been in her home. Maybe it was the faint smell of him that lingered in the air. Whatever it was, it led to some of her wildest dreams yet.

But when she texted him back to thank him or ask how he was, she'd get one-word replies, if that. It was as if he were still barreling across the highway, inscrutable behind his sunglasses and avoiding any and all questions.

Where was the man who'd swept her away to DC? Who couldn't keep his hands off her? The one who helped her live out some of her favorite fantasies? The man who caught her in his arms when she slipped on wet rock rather than let her fall and couldn't bear to let her out of his sight? She missed *that* man.

Maybe she shouldn't be surprised that he hadn't come around. She didn't quite understand what had changed at the Rutherford Foundation gala, but clearly something had. The Rutherfords had been warm and welcoming—but there was no missing the fact that they were Tom's late wife's parents. Maybe it'd messed with his head to see them all together.

If she could talk to the man, she'd reassure him that she wasn't trying to replace his wife. How could she? She'd never be Stephanie—not in looks, not in family history and not in the way she loved Tom.

Because Stephanie had loved a different Tom than the one Caroline had entrusted with her safety—

and quite possibly her heart. Stephanie had loved a younger, more insecure Tom, a man more desperate to prove he belonged in the rarefied DC air. Perhaps Stephanie's Tom hadn't been quite so dangerous, so inscrutable.

That wasn't Caroline's Tom. The man she missed more every single night was unreadable and playful, commanding and commandeering. He could blend seamlessly into a courtroom, a cabin on the high plains and a DC ballroom.

Caroline wanted more than a wild weekend with him and, despite the ghosting, she was sure he wanted more, too. She just had no idea when she might get it because, aside from the flowers she'd received almost two months ago—and the constant sweeps of her home and office—she had no other indication that there was any sort of nefarious activity happening. She got up, exercised and went to work. She came home and slept. Then she did it all again.

Which was fine. Being with Tom had been a whirlwind of impulse and attraction, one that had led her to take crazy risks. At least there hadn't been any lasting consequences from her time with Tom—except that she missed him.

All she could do was hope that he missed her, too.

Ironically enough, a few weeks after she called in sick to work, she started to get sick for real. She'd been feeling draggy, which she'd chalked up to the stress of, well, *everything*. She had no idea where she stood, both with the corruption case and with a certain FBI agent.

She slept more on the weekends, but she couldn't get caught up with her rest. Then she got sick to her stomach in court and barely called a recess in time to make it to the bathroom. Afterward, she felt fine. It must have been something she ate? She threw out the rest of the chicken salad she'd taken for lunch. It smelled funny.

Then the same thing happened the next day—she felt fine until right after lunch, when her stomach twisted. Again, it was a close call, but she made it to the bathroom in time. As she sat on the floor, waiting for her stomach to settle, she realized something.

It hadn't been the chicken salad.

She'd been tired. Now she was sick, but not with the flu or anything. Caroline did the math. It'd been three weeks since her whirlwind weekend with Tom. And her period…

Oh, *crap.*

She should have gotten her period last week.

Caroline was sick again. The whole time, she kept thinking, *No.*

No, no, no, *no.* This couldn't be happening, not again. She'd dodged this bullet once before. She'd missed a period due to stress and it'd made her see that she shouldn't marry Robby, that she couldn't prove her stupid brother right—she wasn't a mistake.

Oh, God. She'd lost her head and her heart to Tom Yellow Bird. For one amazing weekend, she'd thrown all caution to the wind and put her selfish wants and needs before rational thought and common sense.

Had she really been stupid enough to think she'd managed to avoid the consequences of her actions?

Idiot. That's what she was. Hadn't she learned that anytime she stepped outside the safety of making the correct choices—*every* time—fate would smack her down?

Now she was most likely carrying Tom's child.

Oh, *God.*

She sat on the floor of the bathroom, the tile cool against her back, and tried to think. The first time her period had been late, all the way back in college, her life had flashed before her eyes. She'd been terrified of telling Robby, then her parents. They would have gotten married and she would've had to notify the law school that she'd have to defer a year—or withdraw completely. Her career prospects, all of her plans—all of it would have been wiped away by a positive test result. She'd been sick then, too—but with sheer dread as she waited on the pregnancy test results.

No. She'd known it then and she knew it even better now. Marrying Robby and having his baby would have been the biggest mistake of her life.

Now? Oh, she was still panicking. Unplanned potential pregnancies were an anxiety attack waiting to happen.

But instead of filling her with dread, this time when her life flashed before her eyes, she felt...hopeful. Which was ridiculous, but there it was.

She saw her body growing heavy with Tom's baby. Instead of ghosting through her life, she saw Tom coming home to her at the end of the day, cuddling a little baby with his dark hair and eyes. She saw nights in his arms and trips to visit both his friends on the reservation and the Rutherfords and…

Oh, no.

She wanted that life with Tom. She didn't want this to be a mistake.

She needed to talk to him immediately. Or, at the very least, as soon as she had peed on a stick.

Okay. She had a plan. After work, she'd go buy a pregnancy test. And then she was tracking down Tom Yellow Bird if it was the last thing she did.

"Judge Jennings."

The silky voice pulled her out of musing about baby names in the parking lot on her way home from work that day. She found herself standing a few feet away from a man in a good suit wearing mirrored sunglasses. But it wasn't Tom. This guy was white with light brown hair that he wore stylishly tousled. He was tall and lean—much taller than she was—but due to the cut of the suit, she could tell he had plenty of muscles.

He could've been attractive, but there was something in the way his mouth curved into a smirk that she didn't like. Actually, that wasn't strong enough. There was something about this guy that was physically repulsive.

"Yes?" she said, trying to gauge how far she was from her car without actually looking at it. Too far. She'd have to go back into the courthouse. Which was fine. The security guards were still there and they were armed.

"I'm glad we've finally met," the stranger said, his smirk deepening. "I've been looking forward to getting acquainted with you for quite some time now."

Oh, crap. "If that was supposed to sound not creepy, I have to tell you, it didn't make it." She smiled sympathetically, as if he were socially awkward and doing the best he could instead of scaring her.

"Excellent," he said, the smirk widening into a true grin. "A sense of humor. It makes everything so much easier, don't you think?"

Oh, she didn't like that smile at all. She took a step back. If she kicked out of her heels, she could run a lot faster. And screaming was always a viable option.

The man straightened. "Relax, Judge Jennings. Did you enjoy the flowers?"

Double crap. She was starting to panic—but even in the middle of that, James Carlson's last email came back to her. *If they reach out to you, play along.* So she straightened and stood her ground, trying to look like she was the kind of woman who could be swayed by several hundred dollars' worth of cut flowers. "They were lovely, actually. Am I to thank you for that?"

He waved the suggestion away. "I must say you are a very difficult woman to get a handle on," he said, as if he had a right to get a handle on her at all. "I have been deeply impressed by your record on the bench."

How was she supposed to play along when he was making her skin crawl? She couldn't. "Still creepy," she said, backing up another step. "If you'd like to make an appointment to discuss something of merit, feel free to call my assistant and schedule a time.

Other than that? I don't think we have anything to talk about here."

"Oh, but we do. We do, Judge Jennings," he repeated, because apparently annoying was just a way of life for this guy. "It would be such a shame to see a fine judicial career destroyed because of one naive mistake, don't you agree?"

The world stopped spinning. At least, that was how it felt to Caroline as she suddenly struggled to keep her balance. "What? I don't know what you're talking about." The protest sounded weak, even to her own ears. "I don't make mistakes."

He advanced on her, two quick steps. She tensed, but he didn't touch her. She couldn't run, though—she could barely hold herself upright.

"Excellent," he said again. He was overly fond of that word. "Then the Verango case was intentional, was it? Terrence Curtis was your mentor, after all. It's funny how these things work out, isn't it?" He said that last part so softly Caroline almost leaned forward to catch the last words.

She didn't dare. "I've had a lot of cases," she said, wondering if she sounded like she was on the verge of blacking out. "I can't say for certain which case you're talking about." It wasn't much of a lie, but it was all she had right now.

Tom had known this was coming. He had warned her, and she had willfully ignored his warning because…

Because she'd thought the shameful truth wouldn't get out. No one had ever drawn a connection between her and Verango, between Verango and Curtis. Because she had convinced herself that there was no connection beyond the mentor and mentee relationship.

"Yes," the man said in what might have been an understanding voice coming from anyone else. "I can see that you know exactly what I'm talking about. And won't our mutual friend, FBI Special Agent Tom Yellow Bird, be interested to know about this new development?" He snapped his fingers. "Better yet, I could call James Carlson up and inform him that, despite his hopes and prayers, he has yet another judge to prosecute, hmm?"

"What do you want?" she demanded, trying to sound mean and failing miserably.

"Not much," he said, his tone giving lie to his words. "Merely an exchange. I keep your unfortunate mistake between you and me—like friends do—and in exchange, when a case of interest to me comes before you, you'll give me a moment of your time to make my case." His mouth tightened, and Caroline was afraid that was the real guy, finally cracking through the too-perfect exterior. "Although I won't be scheduling an appointment with your assistant. I'm thinking more along the lines of...dinner?"

"You want me to throw a case?" On some level—the logical, rational level—she knew this was great. This was exactly the break that Tom and James Carlson had been waiting for. Whoever was buying off judges was actively trying to blackmail her!

But there was nothing great about this. Not a

damned thing. "He can't watch you forever, no matter how hard he might try," the man said, leaning forward and finally letting the true menace in his voice bleed through. "Do you really want him to know how easily you can be bought?"

There was no need to ask who *he* was.

"No," she whispered, shame burning through her body. Because that was the truth. Tom would find out what she had done all those years ago and it would change things.

Even more than things had already changed. She might be carrying his child.

God, how she didn't want to regret what had happened between her and Tom. She didn't want to regret him. But he might damn well regret her.

Who would want to be saddled with a woman who'd lied by omission about her past, who'd gotten pregnant? She could ruin his career as well as her own. All because she'd lost her head for one weekend.

All because she couldn't say no to Tom Yellow Bird.

Her stomach lurched dangerously, and she fought the urge to cover her belly with her hand. "I don't."

"Excellent," he repeated yet again. "Judge Jennings, it has been a pleasure making your acquaintance." He pulled a business card out of his pocket and held it out to her. But when she went to reach for it, he held it just out of reach. "We understand each other, don't we? Because I would hate to see a promising career like yours destroyed over a little mistake like this."

Caroline swallowed down the bile in the back of her throat. "We understand each other," she agreed. Because she did. Her promising career had indeed been cut short.

She waited for this vile man to say "excellent" again, but he didn't. Instead, he reverted back to a smirk and handed the card over. "If you have any questions or need anything from me—anything at all—I can help you. But only if you help me."

She didn't even look at the card. She slid it into her purse and tried to smile. She didn't know how she would ever smile again. "Of course," she said, impressed that she managed to make it sound good.

With a nod of his head, he turned on his heel and walked off. He didn't get into a car. He merely walked away. When he rounded the corner of the courthouse, Caroline counted to five and then followed. If she could get a car, a license plate—something…

But by the time she could see around the corner, he was gone. Not a car in the street, not the back of his head—nothing.

Her stomach rolled. She was going to be sick.

And it was no one's fault but her own.

Fifteen

The only reason Tom didn't leave flowers for Caroline at her house after every time he swept it was because he didn't want to freak her out. After all, she didn't exactly have positive associations with random floral displays in South Dakota.

But he was tempted. After the initial sweep, he hadn't found any other bugs in her house or office. Which was good. He probably didn't need to be checking things on a regular basis. He should return her key to her. But he couldn't stop. He had to make sure she was safe.

But it was the only thing he could do while keeping his distance. In the meantime, he and Carlson waited for the other players to make their next moves. He knew from a career of waiting that counting each tick of the clock wouldn't make it move a damned bit faster.

He hated not having the ball in his court. Whoever had bugged her house knew that Tom had pulled the devices. They probably knew Tom was doing regular checks. And it was safe to assume that the bad guys had put two and two together and knew that Tom and Caroline had spent at least part of that weekend together. They were no doubt plotting their next move, and all Tom could do was wait to react defensively.

The wait was going to kill him. Slowly.

Because he *missed* Caroline. That, in and of itself, was new. He didn't miss people, not like this. The only other person he'd felt this consuming loneliness for was…

Well, Stephanie. But she'd been dead and he'd been grieving the loss. Caroline was pointedly not dead. In fact, she was within an easy drive. All he'd have to do was park in her driveway and knock on the door.

He couldn't. He was on a case—several cases.

As the days passed, he couldn't stop thinking about what Mark Rutherford and Carlson had both said—that maybe it was time to move on. Maybe Tom already had, but he hadn't realized it until the moment he'd seen Caroline across the crowded courtroom.

He'd spent an electric weekend with her. He'd kicked back and relaxed. He'd enjoyed the explosive sex. He'd taken her to meet the Rutherfords. All of those were things he didn't normally do. That was the only thing that was messing with him. He'd tried something new.

That was all it should have been.

But it wasn't. Because he missed her.

He'd wanted…he wasn't even sure what he'd wanted with Caroline. Sweeping her house and keeping his distance wasn't it, though.

If he were being honest, he'd wanted to see her more. A lot more. But doing that would jeopardize the case.

Spending more time with Caroline…

It had felt like a betrayal of Stephanie. But the thing that Tom couldn't get his head around was the fact that no one else seemed to think that. Not Stephanie's parents. Not Carlson—and they'd all known Stephanie for a much longer time than Tom had. Every single one of them had said the same thing—Stephanie would have wanted him to move on.

Was that what Caroline was? Was Tom finally moving on?

These were the thoughts that occupied Tom constantly as the days dragged on. Tom was tracking down a lead on a different case—sadly, crime waited for no man—when his phone buzzed and he answered it. "Yellow Bird."

"Tom." It was Carlson.

Tom felt a flare of hope. Had someone made a move on Caroline? He hoped like hell they had so this case could end—although he was irritated that she would have gone to Carlson instead of him.

Carlson went on, "There's been a development. You need to come in to the office."

"When?"

"Now."

The last of the lunch rush was thinning out, so it only took Tom twenty minutes to make it over to Carlson's office. He called Caroline to make sure she was all right, but she didn't answer.

He had a fleeting moment when he wished that he had called her at some point during the last few weeks or come up with some sort of excuse to stop by the courthouse and see her. Texting hadn't been enough. He knew there were solid reasons why he hadn't. He didn't want anyone to make a connection between them. He didn't want to compromise the case any more than he already had, so he'd kept his distance.

A growing sense of dread was building inside him and he wasn't sure why. A development should be exciting—another step closer to finishing this case and finding out who was behind the corruption. This was what he lived for, right?

As he thought about what he lived for, though, it wasn't slapping cuffs on a dirty judge that came to mind. It was Caroline. The way she looked curled up next to the fire pit, wineglass in hand. The way she looked curled against his chest the next morning, a little smile on her face as she slept.

He could hear Mark Rutherford asking him if the job really was the most important thing. And suddenly he knew—it wasn't. He could give everything he'd ever had and ever would have to the job, but what could it give him in return? The promise of more criminals committing crimes. The certainty that the job would never be done.

The realization that he might have given up his dreams of living a long and happy life with Stephanie, but he hadn't given up those dreams of a home, a family.

A wife.

After this, he was going to take some time off, he decided as he walked into Carlson's office. He needed to start over with Caroline. She was probably furious with him—and she was well within her rights to be so, considering he hadn't seen her in much too long. But he knew now that he couldn't keep putting the job first, because it would never return the favor.

And then, as if he'd summoned her just by thinking about her, there she was, standing up from the chair in front of Carlson's desk. Carlson, sitting behind the desk, didn't move at all.

Tom blinked a couple of times, trying to make sense of what he was seeing. Caroline was here and his heart gave an excited little leap—but she wasn't happy. There was something wrong—her eyes were red and watery and her mouth was tight. Instinctively, he moved closer to her. "What's going on?"

Something bad had happened—he knew that much. It was physically painful when she turned her gaze to his. The way she was looking at him—it was like someone had killed her puppy. And she didn't have a puppy.

No one said anything. Tom went to her and put his arms around her shoulders. She sagged against him a little as she drew in a shuddering breath, and in that moment, Tom knew he would kill for this woman. Whoever had hurt her, they would pay.

Carlson's face was drawn and worried. He had arranged his features into a stern look, but Tom could tell he was concerned. "Is someone going to tell me what's going on or not?"

"I'm so sorry," Caroline whispered against his chest.

That didn't sound good. In fact, that sounded bad. He held her tighter and glared at Carlson. "Well?"

"As anticipated, someone reached out to Caroline. We have his name and contact number, as well as a description."

"Okay..." That was fine. They'd expected that. "I know they didn't have any bugs in your house and they didn't have anything on you. What were they trying to use for blackmail?"

Caroline shuddered again and then inexplicably pushed him away. She sank down into her chair, staring at the floor as if it held all the answers. "They do have something on me," she said in a voice so torn with anguish that Tom crouched down next to her to catch all of her words.

"What? I checked you out. You're completely clean."

She shook her head. "No. Not completely."

She wouldn't look at him. Why wouldn't she look at him? Anger flared. He'd really like to punch something.

"Caroline has explained the situation," Carlson began. Tom wanted to ignore him, but he was the only one talking and Tom still didn't know what was going on, so he had to pay attention. But he didn't look away from Caroline. Tears dripped down her cheeks, and each one was like a knife in his heart.

"When she was a first-year prosecutor in Minneapolis, her college mentor approached her. He had a friend of a friend who'd been arrested. It was the usual line—the charges were baseless, the friend was really innocent. He pressed Caroline to drop the charges. She wasn't able to do that, but she offered a plea agreement, which led to a suspended sentence and no time served. As a result, her student loans were paid off."

It all sounded so clinical coming of Carlson's mouth. There was a dinner, a conversation. A plea agreement. Loans were paid off.

"How much?"

Carlson didn't answer, and after a moment, Caroline replied, "Almost two hundred thousand dollars." She still wouldn't look at him.

He stood so suddenly that she recoiled in the chair. If he'd been a younger man, Tom would've put his fist through the wall. Maybe even the glass of the door. But he was older and wiser and he knew that breaking his hand wouldn't solve any of life's problems.

No matter how good it might feel.

"They're counting on her doing anything to keep that series of events quiet," Carlson went on. "The fact that she has come forward to voluntarily share this information before allowing it to compromise yet another case is to be commended. She also detailed how, over the years, she's donated a comparative amount to various charities—including the Rutherford Foundation—in an attempt to make restitution."

Tom glared at his friend. Carlson was trying to make this sound good—but there was no way to put lipstick on this pig. Caroline had lied to him. He had asked her—repeatedly—if there was anything in her history that could be used against her. Okay, maybe most of that conversation had gotten distracted by sex—but he had asked. She had said no.

Not only had she lied to him, but…

She could be bought.

He didn't just want to punch something. He wanted to shoot something. Repeatedly.

Because they were supposed to be equals. One of the things that made them good together was the fact that they both took their jobs seriously and upheld the law. They didn't throw cases, they didn't accept bribes and they didn't subvert justice.

"Tom," Carlson said, his voice more severe this time, "it was a long time ago. And since that time, Judge Jennings has upheld the law with honor and dignity."

He knew what Carlson was trying to do. He knew what Carlson wanted—he wanted Caroline to play along. He wanted her to find out more information not just about the man who had approached her, but about who that man was working for. He wanted to use Caroline.

Tom's vision narrowed, growing into a murky red around the edges. "Is there anything else?" His voice sounded wrong even to his own ears.

Panic clawed at the edge of his awareness, because he knew this feeling. *Nothing.* He felt nothing.

It was the same horrifying numbness that had overtaken him as he'd stood next to his wife's bed in the hospital and watched life slip away from her broken body.

He couldn't afford to feel anything right now, because if he did, he would lose his mind, and there would be no coming back from that.

He'd thought he'd known Caroline. More than that, he'd taken her to his house. He'd introduced her to the Rutherfords. He'd…he'd trusted her. And he'd thought she'd trusted him. But had she, really?

"Actually, there is." Carlson came around the desk. Without further explanation, he walked out of the office and closed the door behind him.

Bad sign. Getting worse.

"Tom, sit. Please." Caroline's voice broke, but it didn't hurt him. It couldn't.

He sat and waited. How much worse could this get?

"You have to understand—I was so young. I was twenty-four, in my first job. I was drowning under the weight of my student loans. I was having trouble sleeping and was falling behind on my bills and…" She covered her mouth with her hand, but he wasn't going to be moved by it. "Terrence Curtis was my mentor. He always pushed me to be better, and I trusted him. He wrote me letters of recommendation and helped me get into law school…"

"Sure. You owed him."

"It wasn't like that," she snapped, sounding a little

more like her old self. Good. He wanted her to fight him about this. He didn't want her to make a pitiful plea. "I should've known better. But he asked me out to dinner to talk about how things were going. I was struggling. We talked and then he mentioned the case that I had coming up—Vincent Verango. He said he knew Vincent personally and it was all a big misunderstanding and he would vouch for the man. And I had no reason not to trust him. I shouldn't have, but I did."

"There's a bit of a gap between trusting a mentor and taking that much cash."

"It wasn't like that," she protested. "He never said, 'If you let my friend off easy, I'll pay off your student loans.' He was too smart for that. I… I was too smart for that. He twisted everything around, and I didn't even know that the loans were going to be paid off until suddenly, they were gone. Vincent was gone, too. Out of state. He's since died, I heard. It was only then that I began to get suspicious. I dug a little deeper and discovered that Vincent had a long list of plea deals and dropped charges—racketeering, money laundering—he was in deep with so much and…and Curtis was in bed with him. Curtis protected him. He used me," she said, sounding angrier by the second. "He knew I trusted him and he used that, and for what?

"God, I was such an idiot but I couldn't see how to undo it without ruining my career. So…" Her anger faded as quickly as it had come on. "I didn't do anything."

"It's a great story, Caroline. I'm not sure any of it's the truth, but it's a great story. You make a very convincing innocent bystander." The color drained out of her face, but Tom didn't care. "Was there something else you needed to tell me? Because if not, I have things to do."

She looked terrible. Not that he cared anymore, because he didn't. But if he had, he would've been legitimately worried about her. She looked on the verge of passing out. Maybe he would ask Carlson to track down something for her to drink—he couldn't leave her like this.

She didn't answer, which unfortunately gave Tom time to think.

He'd spent years coping with the fact that there would be no happy endings for him, not after Stephanie. And then Caroline Jennings had shown up and given him a glimpse of a different life—of the different man he could be with her.

That was the cruelest thing of all, Tom decided. Just a glimpse at what could've been, and now it was being snatched away.

If she'd never come here and he'd never laid eyes on her, he wouldn't know what he was missing. But now he would. From here on out, every time he went out to his cabin and lay in his bed, he'd think of her, probably for the rest of his life. His miserable, lonely life.

He could definitely shoot something. He'd start with her mentor, work his way through this Vincent guy and then finish off with whoever had confronted her today.

"I'm so sorry," she whispered again.

For some reason, that made him feel like he was the bad guy here when he most definitely wasn't. He had done nothing wrong. Was he yelling? Was he flipping the desk? Was he threatening bodily harm—at least, was he doing it out loud? No. He was doing none of those things. He was politely listening to her tale of woe.

Damn it, he wanted to reassure her that it would be all right. He wasn't going to, but he wanted to. "About the bribe you took, or is this particular apology in regards to something else?"

She moved then, reaching down and pulling her purse into her lap. Her hands were shaking so violently that it took her a few tries to get it unzipped. Tom watched her curiously.

Then she held something out to him. It was a white stick, maybe four inches. One end of it was purple and there was a small digital screen on it.

He blinked. Desperately, he wanted to believe that was a digital thermometer, but he knew better. Jesus, he knew better. Because sometimes, when a girl wanted to get off the streets, it wasn't for her—but for the baby she was carrying. He kept a supply of pregnancy tests in the safe house.

"I..." she said, holding the pregnancy test out to him. "We..."

This wasn't happening. He was hallucinating. Or having a nightmare. Did it matter at this point? No. What mattered was that he had left reality behind and was stuck in some alternative universe, one where his second chance at happiness betrayed his trust and got pregnant with his child at the same time.

He was tempted to laugh because this was crazy. Simply insane. The only reason he didn't was because Caroline was crying and it hurt him. Damn it all to hell.

"We used protection," he said out loud, more to himself than to her. He tried to think, but his brain wouldn't function. Nothing was functioning.

She nodded, wrapping her arms around her waist and curling into a ball. "That's what I thought, too. Then I was tired and then I got nauseous. And I thought…the shower? In DC?"

Jesus, she was pregnant. With his baby, no less. All those dreams of fatherhood that he had put away years ago—they tried to break free and run rampant around his head. He wouldn't let them. He couldn't afford to.

She was right. He'd been so swept up in living out his fantasy of shower sex that he hadn't taken the most basic of precautions. "That's…" He swallowed and then swallowed again. "That's my fault."

She nodded. "Mistakes happen."

He closed his eyes, but that was when all of those hopes broke free. Caroline, in his bed every night. Caroline, her belly rounded with his child. Caroline, nursing their baby while Tom made her dinner. A thousand visions from an everyday, ordinary life flashed before his eyes—a life that, until twenty minutes ago, he had wanted.

But now?

"Why didn't you tell me about the bribe?"

"I put it behind me. No one ever connected Curtis to Verango, much less to me and my student loans." She sighed, looking more like the judge he knew. "I knew it was wrong, but I couldn't go back and undo it. How was I going to unpay the loans? Who would I give the money to, even if I could come up with that much cash?" She shook her head. "It's not a good excuse, and I know it. But I figured that, since no one had made the connection, no one ever would. I didn't..." She sniffed and Tom got a glimpse of the younger woman she'd been, trying so hard to be an adult and not quite making it. "I didn't want to own up to my poor judgment. But more than that, I didn't want you to think less of me.

"But now that it's out in the open, I wanted to tell you, because I knew that if you could just see that I'd been young and stupid, you would do what you always do."

"And what do I always do, Caroline?" It came out more gently than he'd intended.

She looked up at him, her eyes wide and trusting. "You protect me, Tom. You keep me safe."

He stood and turned away, because he couldn't be sure what expression was on his face right now. Damn it all. He wasn't supposed to care about her at all. She was a part of an ongoing investigation. That should have been the extent of it.

Except now she was pregnant. With his child. Because he hadn't done his goddamn job and put the case first.

He'd put *her* first.

"I didn't... I mean..." She made a hiccuping noise that about broke his heart. "I understand if this is a deal breaker, of course. But it was never malicious. And I *never* meant to hurt you."

She was making this worse. "How long ago was this?"

"Almost thirteen years ago."

He dropped his head in his hands. Thirteen years ago, Stephanie had still been alive. He hadn't yet let her walk out of that party alone. He had desperately been trying to prove that he was good enough for her and wondering if he would ever feel like he belonged.

He turned to face Caroline. God, even now, meeting her gaze was a punch to the gut. "Anything else I should know?"

She nodded tearfully. "I had a pregnancy scare in college. With the guy I almost got engaged to. I was... I was terrified. I hadn't been careful enough. I'd made a serious mistake, and I realized when it happened that I didn't love the guy. And I was going to have to marry him and it was going to kill my career aspirations and my parents were going to be so disappointed in me. They'd finally see what my stupid brother had been saying for years, that I was a mistake."

He was going to shoot her brother if he ever got the chance.

But more than that, each word was like a knife to his chest. Yeah, he could see how an unplanned pregnancy would have changed the course of her life back then.

Just like it could do right now.

"What happened?" he asked in a strangled voice.

"I was just late. It was the stress of senior year." She tried to smile, as if she wanted to display how relieved she was. "I didn't want anyone to know, because it was a serious lapse in judgment and if I couldn't make the right choices to avoid something entirely preventable, like an unplanned pregnancy, then why should anyone take me seriously as a professional?"

"Right, right." He looked down at the little stick. "This isn't just stress, is it?"

She shook her head. "I'm so sorry."

Yeah, he was sorry, too. It would be easy to blame her for this, but hell—she didn't get pregnant by herself. "I'm almost afraid to ask—but anything else?"

"No. I made a serious error in judgment my first year as prosecutor and I'm pregnant. I think that's enough for one day." She paused and looked at him, still nervous. "Tom, this guy—he said you couldn't protect me forever."

Tom moved without being conscious of what he was doing. He hauled Caroline out of her seat and crushed her to his chest.

He was mad, yeah—but he couldn't walk away from her. "He doesn't know me very well, then, does he?"

She wept against his chest, and he held her tight. He couldn't help himself.

His trust in her had been misplaced. And maybe he wouldn't get that second chance. But he'd be damned to hell and back before he threw her to the wolves. He protected people.

He was going to protect her.

He stroked the tears away from her cheeks with his thumbs. "I've ruined everything, haven't I?"

She was going to have his baby. She was in real danger. He'd compromised the case. He'd compromised her.

She hadn't ruined anything. He, on the other hand, might have destroyed everything he'd dedicated his life to.

Oh, if only Stephanie could see him now. What would she say? Would she laugh and tell him to relax, like she used to when he got uptight about some fancy shindig in DC? Would she give him that gentle look and tell him he was being an ass?

Or would she tell him that there was more to life than work? That he, more than anyone else, should know not to let life slip through his fingers, because it could all go away tomorrow?

He and Stephanie had always wanted a family. Would she tell him he'd be insane to let this second chance with Caroline pass him by?

A light tap cut off his jumbled thoughts. The door swung open, revealing a very worried Carlson. "Is everything okay in here?"

Tom glared at the man, but he knew he couldn't get rid of him. Not only were they in Carlson's office, they were friends. "Now what?" It came out more of a growl than a question.

"You aren't going to like this," Carlson warned.

Tom tensed, because he knew how far Carlson would go to root out this corruption. Carlson would want Caroline to get closer to her contact and get as much information as she could without endangering herself. He'd want her to wear a wire, maybe flirt—anything to get the information the case needed.

He stared down into Caroline's eyes. How was he supposed protect her—and their child—if she did any of that?

"No," he said, turning his body so that he stood between Caroline and Carlson. "We do this my way or we don't do it at all."

Sixteen

Suddenly, after a career of waiting, Tom didn't have patience for a single damn thing.

This Todd Moffat scum had contacted Caroline and threatened to ruin her career if she didn't go along with what he wanted.

Caroline had withheld the truth from Tom.

She was also carrying his child.

How was he supposed to do anything but spirit Caroline as far away from the likes of Moffat as possible? Worse, how was he supposed to trust her?

The wheels of justice turned mighty slowly. Tracing Moffat took time, as did getting the appropriate warrants. Neither Tom nor Carlson wanted to get a case dismissed on a technicality—especially not about something as important as this. They couldn't rush this just because Tom couldn't sleep, couldn't eat—couldn't breathe.

He'd compromised the case. He'd compromised Caroline.

God, he hoped like hell he hadn't ruined everything.

Yes, it was important, what he was doing. This years-long investigation was connected not only to judicial corruption, but also to environmental rights and tribal sovereignty—all of it was very, *very* important. Damned important, even. Lives hung in the balance.

But he couldn't let what Caroline had said about her so-called mentor go. She'd lied to Tom about her past—but had she lied about what had actually happened? Had she glossed over her real role or had her mentor used her like she'd said he had?

Tom needed to know. He couldn't let it go. It took a few days because he moved through nonofficial channels, but eventually he tracked down the telephone number for one Terrence Curtis.

When Curtis said, "Hello?" in a voice that shook with age, he sounded ancient.

Tom announced himself. When Curtis spoke again, he sounded more confident. "Agent Yellow Bird, how can I help you today?" He did not sound like a suspect trying to hide his guilt.

"I need to ask you a few questions about one of your former students—Caroline Jennings? Do you remember her?" Tom kept his voice level, almost bored.

"Oh, yes—Caroline. One of my best students—and I say that as someone who taught for decades.

We've fallen out of touch, but I've kept up with her career. She's done great things, and I know she'll go on to do even better things."

He sounded like a proud father, not a man who had hoodwinked his best student into abetting a criminal. But the fact that Curtis remembered her fondly made Tom feel a little more kindly toward him. "So you remember her."

"I just said that, Agent Yellow Bird," Curtis said, sounding exactly like a teacher scolding a student. "Is everything all right with Caroline?"

"What can you tell me about the Verango case?" Tom said, hoping to catch Curtis off guard.

"The… I'm sorry," he said quickly. "I'm not sure what you're talking about."

"You're not? That's a shame. Because Caroline, one of your best students, remembers the conversation very clearly. The one where you convinced her to settle for a plea agreement that would let your friend Vincent Verango go free?"

There was a stunned silence on the line, and for a second, Tom thought the old man had hung up on him. He didn't want that to happen. Curtis still lived in Minneapolis and it was a hell of a long drive.

"That's…" Curtis said flatly. "That's not how it happened. Verango and I were not friends. I never—"

"Oh, but you did, didn't you, Mr. Curtis?" Tom cut him off. "It's not a point of contention up for debate. I'm just trying to corroborate her story. Because Caroline, your best student, has done great things, and as you say, she could conceivably continue to do great things from the bench—if her entire career isn't derailed by a corruption scandal. One that traces directly back to *you*."

Curtis made a strangled noise, somewhere between a choke and a gasp. "What—who?"

"All very good questions. Here's what I think, Mr. Curtis. You were her mentor. She looked up to you. She trusted you—maybe she was a little naive about that, but you were both working for the good guys, right?" Silence. "She says that, when she was struggling during her first year as a prosecutor, you took her out to dinner to offer her some moral support. A pep talk. And while you were there, you mentioned you had a friend, Vincent, who had been unfairly arrested. You vouched for him, and as a result of your conversation, Caroline did not throw the book at him. She pulled her punches and Vincent walked." More silence. Man, he really hoped Curtis hadn't hung up on him. "Shortly thereafter, all her student loans were paid off in full. Am I leaving anything out?"

"I..." Curtis sounded older—and definitely more scared.

"And that's why you fell out of touch, isn't it? Because when she figured out that you had abused her trust—it was gone, wasn't it? She kept her distance because it was the only way to protect herself."

"I needed the money," he said, his voice shaking. "I made sure she got a good cut—"

"I don't give a shit what your reasons were. I just need to know whether or not Caroline Jennings was your dupe or if she was an active participant in the miscarriage of justice."

"Of course she didn't know!" Curtis erupted. "I didn't think she'd mind—I was trying to help her out. I should've known better. She always was one of the smartest students I've ever had."

Tom had what he needed—proof that Caroline had not intentionally broken the law. She'd just put her faith in the wrong man.

That pregnancy scare in college, this thing with the Verango case—each time Caroline had slipped up, it was because she'd trusted the wrong man.

And now she was pregnant with Tom's child because she'd believed him. When he'd told her he needed to take her out to his cabin to keep her safe, she'd gone. Same for the trip to Washington. She'd questioned him, sure, but in the end, she'd put her faith in him.

They'd both trusted that what happened at the cabin and then in DC was somehow separate from their jobs.

Well, it wasn't separate anymore.

Tom looked up to where Carlson was listening on another receiver. "Anything else?" He was asking both Curtis and Carlson. Carlson shook his head.

"If you talk to her," Curtis said, sounding tired, "tell her I'm sorry. She was one of my best students, you know."

"I'm sure she was." Tom hung up, feeling almost light-headed. Caroline wasn't a dirty judge. Yeah, she still should have told him about this, way back when he'd asked if there was anything that could be used against her.

But damn it all, he understood that impulse to bury a past mistake. Hadn't he been doing the exact same thing? Ten years of his life focusing on the job so he could justify living while Stephanie had died.

"Well?"

"I think I have everything I need," Carlson said, making some notes. "I wasn't going to charge her—you know that, right?"

"She wouldn't expect any special favors. Neither would I." Tom knew that about her. Justice was blind.

Technically speaking, the job wasn't done. The department was closing in on Moffat, but no arrests had been made yet. There was a part of Tom that wanted to be the one to slap the cuffs on his wrists, to look him in the eye and make sure he knew that Tom Yellow Bird had been the one to serve justice. Finally, after all this time.

That was still important to him. But it wasn't the most important thing. Not anymore.

Caroline was his second chance.

He wasn't going to let the job ruin that for him.

Tom stood. "Do you need me for anything else?"

Carlson smiled knowingly. "No. In fact, if I see you in the office in the next five days, I'll have you arrested. Show your face within the next two days, you'll be shot on sight."

Tom was already heading out the door. He paused only long enough to look back over his shoulder. "Go home to your family. Trust me on this, James—you don't want to miss a single moment."

Because everything could change in a moment.

No one knew that better than he did.

Seventeen

Really, not that much had changed over the last several weeks—at least, not on the surface, Caroline thought as she packed up at the end of yet another ordinary day.

She got up, she walked—instead of jogging, which was her only concession to being pregnant and even then, it had more to do with the crippling summer heat than her physical state. She went to work, she came home and she did it all over again.

She did not run away with Tom. In fact, after their confrontation in Carlson's office, he had all but disappeared off the face of the planet. She couldn't blame him. After all, she'd screwed up. She'd made a series of unfortunate mistakes that had compounded upon each other. She'd done serious damage to both of their careers, and if she knew one thing about Tom, it was that his career was everything to him.

She hadn't talked to her brother, Trent, in years. They'd managed a semi-civil nod across the aisle at Mom's funeral several years ago, but Caroline chalked that up more to the influence of his wife than any sentimentality on Trent's part.

Even though she'd cut him out of her life—and vice versa—his hateful words from when she was just a little girl had never left Caroline. She was a mistake and she ruined everything.

She'd heard it so often, in so many ways, that she'd completely internalized Trent's hatred.

Okay, so—yes. She had screwed up. She'd made mistakes. But that didn't make *her* a mistake any more than her parents having her late in life made her a mistake. She might not have been a planned child, but she knew in her heart that she'd made her parents happy.

Yes, Caroline was now pregnant and it could reasonably be described as a mistake.

But that's not what this child was. No, this child was a gift.

Her brother was a hateful man who had blinded her to the truth—far from being a mistake, Caroline had been a gift to her parents. They'd loved her, even if Trent couldn't.

She hadn't planned for this—not for any of it. She hadn't planned to make love with FBI Special Agent Thomas Yellow Bird. She hadn't planned to have her errors in judgment thrown back in her face when she'd least expected it. She had absolutely not planned to get pregnant.

But, yes—unplanned or not, this child was a gift. That didn't mean she and Tom were going to raise this baby together. Even though she was wishing for exactly that.

Because just like it took two to make a baby, it took two to raise one. Oh, sure, Caroline could do the single-mom thing. Women had been successfully raising babies on their own for millennia. But she didn't want to.

She wanted long drives into the sunset and long weekends at a cabin in the middle of nowhere. She wanted to meet the people Tom had grown up with, and she wanted her child to know his roots. She wanted to spend time with Celine and Mark Rutherford and do what she could for the Rutherford Foundation.

She wanted Tom. All of him, not just the parts that looked good in a suit. She wanted the insecure young man carving out a place for himself where none had previously existed and she wanted the overconfident agent who did what he thought was best, come hell or high water. She wanted the fantastic lover and the man who made sure she had the right clothes for events so she wouldn't be nervous.

And if she couldn't have him—all of him—then...

Then he couldn't have her. She wasn't going to settle for anything less than everything. They'd have to share custody or something.

Frankly, the very idea pissed her off. As did the fact that he still hadn't called. Was that just it, then? She'd lied by omission and he was done with her? If that wasn't the pot calling the kettle black, she didn't know what was. Getting a straight answer out of that man about anything was only accomplished by magic, apparently. He hadn't told her he was taking her to his luxury cabin. He hadn't told her she was going to the Rutherford Foundation gala. He hadn't told her anything until the information became vital.

Was that because she wasn't important enough to trust with the information? Or was it just that the job would always come first?

Deep down, she was afraid she was on her own, because in all honesty, she wasn't sure if Tom would ever be able to put her and the baby before his job. She couldn't replace his late wife, and he lived and breathed being an agent. She might be up against forces beyond her control.

When she finally did see him again, she didn't know if she'd kiss him or strangle him, frankly. It depended heavily upon the hormones.

Caroline was staring at her refrigerator, battling yet another wave of not-morning sickness and trying to decide if there was anything that was going to settle her stomach when someone pounded on her front door.

"Caroline!"

Adrenaline dumped into her system as the fight-or-flight response tried to take hold, because who on earth could be banging on her door at six thirty in the evening? Was it a good guy or a bad guy? She couldn't handle any more bad news.

"Caroline! Are you in there?"

Wait, she knew that voice. She sagged—actually sagged—in relief. *Tom.* He was here. Oh, please, let it be good news. Please let it be that they had arrested all the bad guys in the entire state of South Dakota and—and—

Please let him have come for her.

She peeked through the peephole, just to be sure—but it was him. Alone. She threw open the door and said, "Tom! What are you—" but that was as far as she got because then she was in his arms. He was kissing her and kicking the door shut and walking her into the living room and she knew she needed to push back, find out why he was here. But she couldn't. She had missed him *so* much.

But that wasn't her fault. A flash of anger gave her the strength she needed to shove him back. "What are you doing here?" she demanded, gaping at him. He had a wild light in his eyes she could only pray was a good thing. "The case—"

"Screw the case," he said, pulling her back into his arms. "It doesn't matter."

"How can you say that? Of course it matters. What if someone followed you here? What if someone puts us together?"

He was grinning at her. Grinning! He was in the middle of her living room, cupping her face in his hands and looking down at her like she was telling a joke instead of having a panic attack about what the future held. "They better put us together," he said, touching his forehead to hers. "Babe, I am so sorry."

"For what?" She pulled completely out of his grasp,

because she couldn't think while he was touching her, couldn't formulate words when he was holding her so tenderly. She stomped to the other side of the living room and crossed her arms over her chest. "I'm the one who screwed up, remember? I'm the one who compromised the case because I lied about my past. I'm the one who threw a case all those years ago. I'm the one who lied to you, Tom. Why are *you* apologizing to *me*?"

She was yelling, but she didn't care. He was here. She was happy and furious and saddened all at once. Stupid hormones.

And he was still smiling at her, the jerk! "Why are you smiling at me?" she shouted.

"Have I ever told you that you're beautiful when you're furious?"

That did it. She threw a pillow at him—which, of course, he caught easily. "You're not making any sense!" Her voice cracked and her throat tightened and she was afraid she would start crying, which would be terrible. She might have ruined her career and she might be unexpectedly pregnant, but that didn't mean she wanted to break down in front of him.

"I'm just so glad to see you. But," he added, before she could launch another throw pillow at him, "I actually came to tell you something." He held up his hands in the sign of surrender. "Okay, you screwed up. But you're acting as if no one else has ever made a mistake in the history of the world, and you're wrong. I've screwed up more times than I can count, Caroline. Including with you. I got it into my head if I just kept my distance from you, that would keep you safe. That would also keep me safe. And all it did was make us both miserable. I miss you. I need you."

He fished something out of his pocket and held out his palm to her. "I want to be with you. Not just now, not just for the weekend—for the rest of my life. Because I feel it. I've felt it since the very first second I saw you."

"What—what are you doing?" Was that a ring?

"I'd given up on a happy ending, Caroline. I'd fallen in love once before and had it ripped away from me, and I figured that was it. No happy endings. No family. Just my job. And then you showed up." His eyes looked suspiciously bright as he took a few steps across the room. "I saw you and I felt it again—hope. Desire. *Love.* I hadn't been with a woman since the night before my wife died and then you came along, and suddenly, I couldn't keep my hands off you. And that led to *my* mistake. I had no intention of getting you pregnant, and I had no intention of leaving you alone to deal with it by yourself. I'm sorry that I haven't been here. But if you'll have me, if you'll forgive me, I will always be here for you."

Okay, so she was crying. It didn't mean anything. She wiped the tears out of her eyes and looked down at his hand, which was now before her. It *was* a ring. Of course it was. A perfect ring with a really big round diamond and a bunch of smaller diamonds on the band. It was the kind people wore when they got engaged. When they meant to spend the rest of their lives together.

She looked back up at him, trying to keep it together and failing miserably. "But the case—the job—"

Tom shook his head. "For so long, it was personal. I had to prove I belonged by being better than everyone else, and then, when Stephanie died, I… I didn't have anything left. Everyone in my family had passed. I was a long way from home. All I had was the job, and I gave it everything because it was the only way to make things right."

She didn't like the image of him all alone. "Is that why you've been radio silent for so long? You're making things right?"

Tom pulled her into his arms. He looked tired. Was that because of the job or because of her? "I'm not going to let anyone intimidate or threaten you, Caroline. That's a promise. But I don't have to give everything to the job. Not if it keeps me from you." He rested his free hand on her belly. "Not if it keeps me from *this*. I've missed you so much, Caroline. You mean everything to me and I've let you down. If you give me another chance, I won't let you down again."

She swiped madly at the tears rolling down her cheeks, but they were replaced too quickly. "I missed you, too," she sobbed. "I've missed you so much."

Unexpectedly, he fell to his knees. "Caroline Jennings, will you marry me? Because you will always be more to me than a case or a job. I love you. I have from the very first. And I want to spend the rest of my life proving it to you."

She tried to look stern, but it wasn't happening.

"I don't want this to happen again," she told him, starting to hiccup. "I don't want you to disappear for days and weeks on end. I don't want you to leave me alone, wondering..."

"I won't. It was a mistake to do so. But," he went on, climbing to his feet and holding her hands in his, "I have one thing I need to tell you."

She groaned. "What now?"

"I spoke with Terrence Curtis." She gasped, but he just kept going. "He admitted that he convinced you to amend the charges and that you had no idea he had an ulterior motive. He also told me to tell you that he's proud of everything you've accomplished since then. You were one of his best students."

"You tracked down Mr. Curtis for me?"

Tom had said he would protect her. She'd always assumed he meant physically—safe from bad guys and evildoers.

But this? This was her reputation. Her career. And he'd protected it.

"I wanted it on the record that you hadn't intentionally or maliciously broken the law. Carlson won't be pressing charges, either."

"What about..."

"Moffat? We're building the case. We know who he is and who he's working for. We've got him—thanks to you."

She stared at him, because that was all she could do. There weren't any words.

He was back to grinning wildly at her. "Say yes, Caroline. Be my wife, my family. Our family," he added, stroking her stomach. Instantly, the air between them heated, and she felt that spark catching fire again as his hand drifted lower and then higher. She burned for his touch—but with fewer clothes. A lot fewer clothes.

"I took a couple of days off," he murmured. "Let me show you how much I love you."

"Yes." Yes to it all—to his touches, to his proposal, to his love. "I love you, too. But I'm going to hold you to your promises, okay?"

"I'm counting on it."

She couldn't stop the tears, but she smiled anyway as she pulled him into her. "Good. Because I feel it, too. And I'm never letting you go."

Epilogue

Once upon a time, Tom had considered tracking down criminals and arresting them to be difficult but rewarding work. It involved a lot of sleepless nights and hours of patiently waiting for a few moments of intense activity—the arrest—and then, much later, the payoff, a guilty verdict.

All in all, it had been remarkably good training for being a parent.

"Never thought I'd see the day," James Carlson said. Carlson was speaking to Tom, but his gaze was fastened on his wife.

Maggie sat next to the fire pit with Rosebud Armstrong, Celine Rutherford and Caroline. The women were laughing and chatting, all while Maggie rubbed her pregnant belly. Everyone was hoping to make it through this Memorial Day barbecue without the untimely arrival of the second Carlson child.

"See what?" Tom kept an eye on Margaret as she picked up leaves and handed them to Caroline. Tom knew his thirteen-month-old daughter could sit in one place for a while sometimes—but not when Carlson's two-year-old, Adam, was chasing the Armstrong boys around. The twins, Tanner and Lewis, were almost seven and didn't have time for a two-year-old. Instead, Rosebud and Dan's kids were splashing in the spring-fed pool. Poor Adam kept getting soaked, but instead of fussing, he was giving as good as he got, giggling the whole time. Dan Armstrong was nearby, keeping the kids safe in the shallow water.

Margaret watched the whole scene with fascination, and Tom knew it wouldn't be much longer before she tried to follow the older boys into the water. It didn't matter that she could barely walk, much less run. She'd be after them in moments, shrieking with joy. She was such a happy baby. Just looking at her made Tom's heart swell with joy.

"You," Carlson laughed, taking a long pull on his beer as he flipped a buffalo burger.

Tom gave his old friend a dull look. "You see me all the time." Margaret pushed herself to her feet, almost falling into Caroline's legs. Although Caroline kept her attention focused on Rosebud—who appeared to be telling a story about the twins' most recent exploits—she easily caught her daughter and cuddled the baby to her chest.

For years, Tom had waited. He and Stephanie had

wanted to make sure they had their careers set before they took time off to have a family, and then… it'd been too late. He'd figured that he missed his window and fatherhood wasn't in the cards for him.

He had never been more thrilled to be wrong as he was right now.

"No," Mark Rutherford said, watching all the children, "I know what he means. We never thought we'd see you this *happy* again."

Caroline looked up and caught him watching her. And, just like he always had, Tom felt that spark between them jump to life. Every time he saw her, he fell in love with her all over again.

"Yes," Carlson laughed, flipping another burger. "Just like that."

Tom didn't know how to respond to that. He was in uncharted territory here. In addition to being a Memorial Day party, this barbecue at his cabin also marked the end of the corruption investigation that he and Carlson had pursued for years. It also potentially marked the end of Tom's full-time commitment with the FBI. The job was finally done, hopefully permanently.

Todd Moffat had been arrested, tried and convicted. His employer had been revealed to be Black Hills Mines, a mining company that had been locked in several protracted legal battles with the various tribes over uranium rights. Uranium mining was a dirty business, but there were huge deposits underneath the land that made up many of the reservations in South Dakota. Black Hills Mines wanted the right to strip the uranium out of the ground. Understandably, the tribes preferred not to have their reservations destroyed and contaminated. Moffat had turned in favor of a lighter sentence and everything had fallen into place.

The job was over—for Tom, anyway. He was taking a leave of absence from the agency. He'd continue to be available as a consultant—he was still the best agent to deal with cases that involved tribal issues. But he was turning his attention to the Rutherford Foundation.

They were building a new school on the Red Creek Reservation. Tom was going to make sure it was everything his tribe needed.

So this wasn't a farewell party. The agency had gotten him a cake for that at the office. This?

This was a welcome home party. Margaret was at a really amazing age, and he couldn't bring himself to spend his nights sitting in a surveillance vehicle in the hopes that the bad guy did something when he could be at home with his wife and his daughter.

However, no matter how perfect this moment or any of the moments in the previous twenty-three months had been, he knew he didn't have all the time in the world. Maybe he was jaded, but he knew better than anyone else that it could all end tomorrow and he wouldn't waste another moment on something as impersonal as a career. His career would never love him back. It would never give him a family or those thousands of small moments every day that made up a good life.

Margaret was going to start running and talking soon. And Tom was going to be there to see it with his own eyes. He was going to show his little girl the world—powwows and parties and everything that made him who he was, everything that would make her who she was, too.

For years, he'd made his own family—finding members of his tribe and others who were lost and needed a way home. And he hadn't given that up. He might have stepped aside from his job, but he would never turn his back on those who needed him. He had a charity to run, scholarships to fund and people to help. But he didn't need a badge to do that. Not anymore.

He just needed to know that, at the end of a long day, Caroline was coming home to him. She'd returned to her seat on the bench once her maternity leave had ended, and Tom was proud of what she'd accomplished.

Margaret looked up at him and smiled, her fingers in her mouth. She'd probably be up late tonight, fussing at her sore teeth. But right now, she grinned at him and all Tom could think was, there she was—the most perfect little girl in the world.

It was different, the love he felt when he looked at his daughter. It was full of hope and protection and sweetness, whereas when he looked at his wife, it was full of longing and heat and want. But it was love all the same.

"She would have been happy for you," Carlson

said, shaking Tom out of his thoughts. "This was what she'd have wanted for you. You know that, right?"

Tom looked at his wife and daughter and fell in love again, just like he did a hundred times a day. Some days—like right now—he thought his heart might burst from it.

When he'd first fallen for Caroline, he'd struggled to give his heart to her completely. But he knew now—loving Caroline and Margaret didn't take away from the love he'd felt for Stephanie. It didn't make him less. It only made him more. So much more.

"Yeah," he said, staring at the loves of his life. "Yeah, I do."

"We should get a picture," Rosebud called out. "Something to mark the retirement of one of the best special agents the FBI has ever seen."

Everyone agreed, even though it felt like overkill to Tom. He was still adjusting to this new reality, where he wanted people to take pictures of him and his family—wedding pictures and baby pictures he didn't hide in a storage closet, but displayed on the walls of his cabin. He'd paved the road down to the cabin and done away with the shrubbery hiding the turnoff. He didn't have to hide who he was anymore. He belonged, just as he was.

It took time to wrangle all of the kids. Dan had a new tripod for his phone, so he was able to set it up to take a photo of all of them.

Tom's throat tightened as he watched his family and friends arrange themselves around him. Caroline leaned into him, her touch a reassurance. "Okay?" she asked in a quiet voice meant just for his ears.

He stared down at his wife and knew that later, after everyone had left and Margaret had fallen asleep—at least for a few hours—he'd take the spark that had always existed between them and fan it into a white-hot flame. Because he had known from the very beginning—there she was, the woman he was going to spend the rest of his life with.

He kissed her, a promise of things to come, because he would never be done falling in love with her. "I've never been better."

* * * * *

If you loved PRIDE AND PREGNANCY,
pick up these other connected novels from
RITA Award–winning author Sarah M. Anderson.

A MAN OF HIS WORD
Dan and Rosebud's story.

A MAN OF PRIVILEGE
James and Maggie's story.

Available now from Harlequin Desire!

And check out these other books
from Sarah M. Anderson.
A REAL COWBOY
NOT THE BOSS'S BABY
THE NANNY PLAN

* * *

If you're on Twitter, tell us what you think of
Harlequin Desire! #harlequindesire

COMING NEXT MONTH FROM

Available May 9, 2017

#2515 THE MARRIAGE CONTRACT

Billionaires and Babies • by Kat Cantrell

Longing for a child of his own, reclusive billionaire Des marries McKenna in name only so she can bear his child, but when complications force them to live as man and wife, the temptation is to make the marriage real...

#2516 TRIPLETS FOR THE TEXAN

Texas Cattleman's Club: Blackmail • by Janice Maynard

Wealthy Texas doctor Troy "Hutch" Hutchinson is the one who got away. Now he's back and ready to make things right, but Simone is already expecting three little surprises of her own...

#2517 LITTLE SECRET, RED HOT SCANDAL

Las Vegas Nights • by Cat Schield

Superstar Nate Tucker has no interest in the spoiled pop princess determined to ensnare him, but when a secret affair with her quiet sister, Mia, results in a baby on the way, he'll do whatever it takes to claim Mia as his.

#2518 THE RANCHER'S CINDERELLA BRIDE

Callahan's Clan • by Sara Orwig

When Gabe agrees to a fake engagement with his best friend, Meg, he doesn't expect to fight temptation at every turn. But a makeover leads to the wildest kiss of his life and now he wants to find out if friends make the best lovers...

#2519 THE MAGNATE'S MARRIAGE MERGER

The McNeill Magnates • by Joanne Rock

Matchmaker Lydia Whitney has been secretly exacting revenge on her wealthy ex-lover, but when he discovers her true identity, it's his turn to exact the sweetest revenge...by making her his convenient wife!

#2520 TYCOON COWBOY'S BABY SURPRISE

The Wild Caruthers Bachelors • by Katherine Garbera

What happens in Vegas should stay there, but when Kinley Quinten shows up in Cole's Hill, Texas, to plan a wedding, the groom's very familiar brother's attempts to rekindle their fling is hindered by a little secret she kept years ago...

YOU CAN FIND MORE INFORMATION ON UPCOMING HARLEQUIN® TITLES, FREE EXCERPTS AND MORE AT WWW.HARLEQUIN.COM.

HDCNM0417

SPECIAL EXCERPT FROM

HARLEQUIN® Desire

Superstar Nate Tucker has no interest in the spoiled pop princess determined to ensnare him, but when a secret affair with her quiet sister, Mia, results in a baby on the way, he'll do whatever it takes to claim Mia as his.

Read on for a sneak peek at
LITTLE SECRET, RED HOT SCANDAL
by Cat Schield

Mia had made her choice and it hadn't been him.

"How've you been?" He searched her face for some sign she'd suffered as he had, lingering over the circles under her eyes and the downward turn to her mouth. To his relief she didn't look happy, but that didn't stop her from putting on a show.

"Things have been great."

"Tell me the truth." He was asking after her welfare, but what he really wanted to know was if she'd missed him.

"I'm great. Really."

"I hope your sister gave you a little time off."

"Ivy was invited to a charity event in South Beach and we extended our stay a couple days to kick back and soak up some sun."

Ivy demanded all Mia's time and energy. That Nate had spent any alone time with Mia during Ivy's eight-week stint on his tour was nothing short of amazing.

They'd snuck around like teenage kids. The danger of getting caught promoted intimacy. And at first, Nate found the subterfuge amusing. It got old fast.

It had bothered Nate that Ivy treated Mia like an employee instead of a sister. She never seemed to appreciate how Mia's kind and thoughtful behavior went above and beyond the role of personal assistant.

"I don't like the way we left things between us," Nate declared, taking a step in her direction.

Mia took a matching step backward. "You asked for something I couldn't give you."

"I asked for you to come to Las Vegas with me."

"We'd barely known each other two months." It was the same excuse she'd given him three weeks ago and it rang as hollow now as it had then. "And I couldn't leave Ivy."

"She could've found another assistant." He'd said the same thing the morning after the tour ended. The night after Mia had stayed with him until the sun crested the horizon.

"I'm not just her assistant. I'm her sister," Mia said, now as then. "She needs me."

I need you.

He wouldn't repeat the words. It wouldn't do any good. She'd still choose obligation to her sister over being happy with him.

And he couldn't figure out why.

HDEXP0417